FLIGHT
OF THE
FALCON

Susan Geason was born in Tasmania, grew up in Queensland, and now lives in Sydney. Most of her professional life has centred on politics and writing, including positions as a researcher in Parliament House, Canberra and Cabinet Adviser in the NSW Premier's Department. Since 1988 she has worked as a freelance writer and editor, including a six-year stint from 1992–1997 as literary editor of Sydney's *Sun-Herald*. Her crime fiction for adults has been published around the world in several languages. Her first book for teenagers, *Great Australian Girls* (1999), was very successful, and was followed by a companion volume, *Australian Heroines* (2001). Her most recent books are *All Fall Down* and *Death of a Princess*.

She recently completed a PhD in Creative Writing at the University of Queensland.

Susan can be contacted by email: susan@susangeason.com

FLIGHT

OF THE

FALCON

SUSAN GEASON

LITTLE HARE

Little Hare Books
8/21 Mary Street, Surry Hills
NSW 2010 AUSTRALIA

www.littleharebooks.com

First published in 2006

National Library of Australia
Cataloguing-in-Publication entry

  Geason, Susan, 1946– .
  Flight of the falcon.

  For children aged 10+.

  ISBN 1 921049 36 7.

  1. Middle Ages – Juvenile fiction. I. Title.

  A823.3

Cover design by Serious Business
Cover images courtesy of Konstantinos Dafalias (girl) and Jon Stout (castle)
Set in 13.5/17.5pt Adobe Garamond by Asset Typesetting Pty Ltd
Printed and bound in China by Cheong Ming
5 4 3 2 1

This one is for Susie, Sabrina and Simon Woods-Giordano

CHAPTER ONE

It was a glorious September day, sunny with a cool breeze which warned that winter was on its way. Sybilla de Saint-Valery and her younger cousin Raymond had taken advantage of Aunt Maud's busyness to slip away and go hawking in the hills around the castle in Rouen. Sybilla needed a break from her aunt and Raymond was always up for an adventure.

As soon as she had escaped from the watchful eyes in the castle, Sybilla had taken off her constricting veil. Now she removed her falcon's little leather hood and cast him from her wrist. Higher and higher Merlin spiralled until he was just a small speck against the sun. From below he looked terribly small and vulnerable. Sybilla scanned the horizon anxiously, on the lookout for the predators that patrolled the skies of Normandy. Merlin was fast, but gyrfalcons and peregrines were bigger and more powerful.

Sybilla was distracted by a shout from Raymond, who was losing a tug of war with Hannibal, her bloodhound. At twelve — two years younger than Sybilla — Raymond was knobbly-kneed and gangly, with a shock of untidy fair hair that fell into his eyes and drove his mother mad. He had a lively, mischievous nature, but he was also clever and curious, and made it his business to get to know everybody who entered the castle and winkle out their secrets. Sybilla thought him great fun, but unfortunately he never knew when to stop. "Raymond, if Hannibal tears my cloak, we'll be punished," she shouted.

"You will, you mean," Raymond said, taking his eyes off Hannibal for an instant. He should have known better. The bloodhound immediately dropped his end of the cloak, and the boy fell backwards with a thump. Barking joyfully, Hannibal leapt on him and began licking his face. Laughing, Raymond pushed the hound off and clambered to his feet, brushing grass off his breeches. "You know my mother dotes on me, Sybilla," he said, grinning.

Raymond was right. Maud de Barneville treated her son like a prince. Girls, on the other hand, were to be scolded and slapped and turned into obedient, dutiful wives.

2

Sybilla forgot Raymond when the bells on Merlin's legs jangled, and looked up to see the falcon swoop upon a hapless sparrow. Feathers flew. Sybilla was glad she could not hear the small bird's screams. But there was no point in being sentimental about it; hawks had to eat, just as sparrows did. Carrying the small carcass triumphantly in his claws, Merlin descended, straight as an arrow and just as swift, and perched on her leather gauntlet.

"Good bird, Merlin," Sybilla cooed, and fed him the sparrow.

A cloud obscured the sun and, looking up, Sybilla realised that it was getting late. She looked around for Raymond. *You can't take your eyes off the boy for a minute, or he'll be in the next county,* she thought, exasperated. There he was, off in the distance running with Hannibal. "Come back, Raymond!" she yelled. They had to get home before they were missed. The pair were not allowed out in open country without an armed escort — it was too perilous.

The knights of Normandy had been at each other's throats for decades, warring over land and titles, and the children of two noble families would make valuable hostages. Some of these knights were loyal to the Duke of Normandy, under whose protection Sybilla and Raymond lived, while others owed fealty to his younger brother, the King of England. But these alliances shifted constantly, and someone who had been your friend yesterday could be your enemy tomorrow. Sybilla knew that she and Raymond were taking a risk by leaving the castle, but no one could be spared to accompany them, and the day was so beautiful that they had been unable to resist. Besides, Sybilla felt sorry for Merlin, cooped up in the castle's falcon house.

Sybilla had been living in the Duke of Normandy's castle in Rouen for three years now. Her uncle, Raymond's father, was the Duke's steward, so he and his family lived in an apartment in the palace rather than at their estate in Barneville. Before Sybilla's father had despatched her to the castle at Rouen to live with his sister's family, he had given her several rules to follow. The first was to say her prayers every night; the second was to obey her aunt and uncle in all things; and the third was not to gossip or carry tales. Finally, he had warned her: "Make no enemiés, but make no friends either, Sybilla." That had sent a chill creeping down Sybilla's spine. The Duke's courtiers would not see her as a person, her father had explained, but as a pawn in their own quest for power. It was too dangerous to befriend anyone in the castle but her own kin.

Sybilla had wondered how she would survive in such a hostile environment, and longed to stay home where she was safe and loved. But she knew she had to go: all the noble families sent their children off to the castles of their allies to be trained for their roles in life. The boys learned to become knights, and the girls to be fine ladies. Sybilla herself had to learn the etiquette and court protocol required to become a good wife and noblewoman. That meant endless hours spent doing fine stitching and embroidery, learning how to address nobles of different ranks and make polite conversation in company, polishing up her chess and, most importantly, learning from Aunt Maud how to run a household. When Sybilla married, she would have to help run an estate. As well as bringing up her children, she would have to make sure her family and servants were fed and clothed, and supervise the castle's farm, especially the dairy. As the lady of the manor, it was her responsibility to give alms to the poor and make donations to the church. And when her husband went off to war, she would have to run the property in his place with the help of the bailiff.

The very thought of another afternoon of stitching made Sybilla want to stay away from the castle forever, but she had no choice. Sighing, she tethered Merlin's leg bracelets to the ring on her glove with a leather thong and replaced his hood. When he had settled, she called Hannibal and mounted Dancer, her mare, who had been calmly cropping the grass nearby. Raymond jumped up on his horse, and they set off for home.

After galloping for a few leagues across the Duke's vast estate, they crested a hill and saw the castle looming in the distance. It was an impressive sight, soaring into the sky and casting a great shadow over the countryside. Unlike most of the wooden castles that dotted the Norman countryside, the Duke's castle was built of stone and was heavily fortified. Once its massive drawbridge was raised, the moat that surrounded it made it impregnable. If threatened, the Duke's soldiers could rain down boiling oil, fire and stones upon the enemy below, while his archers could let loose wave upon wave of sharp, deadly arrows. Sybilla could see the sun glinting off the weapons of the guards who were patrolling the battlements keeping watch for strangers.

As they began to descend the hill, one of the Duke's guardsmen came thundering across the drawbridge and galloped out along the road. When he caught sight of the pair, he drew his horse to an abrupt halt, and beckoned to them.

"Now we're in for it," groaned Raymond. "Mama must have noticed we were gone."

Dreading the reception that awaited them in the castle, they spurred their horses on to join the guardsman.

"Lady de Barneville sent me, milord and milady," he said. "You're to come with me. It's urgent."

The cousins exchanged looks, anticipating a whipping for Raymond and bed without dinner for Sybilla, and followed the man back to the castle in silence. Once inside the walls, they handed their horses over to the grooms. Normally, Sybilla would groom Dancer herself, but she dared not keep her aunt waiting. Moving quickly, she returned Merlin to the falcon house where he lived with the Duke's gyrfalcons, the peregrines of the courtiers and the squires' lannerets. He squawked in protest and flapped his wings. "Softly, softly, my little birdie," she crooned, and the raptor calmed a little.

With Hannibal trotting obediently at their heels,

the cousins went inside to look for Maud de Barneville. They found her in the Great Hall, seated at one of the long tables, deep in conversation with the bailiff. When she noticed them hovering, Maud signalled them over. Reluctantly, they obeyed. But to their surprise she seemed relieved rather than angry. "Thank God you're safe! I've got very bad news. We've just heard that the Duke's brother, King William of England, is mobilising his troops to cross the Channel and attack Normandy."

Sybilla was speechless with shock, but Raymond seemed to find the news exciting. "When will they be here, Mama?" he asked, his eyes sparkling.

"A matter of days, I should imagine," said Maud. When Raymond started to question her further, she raised her hand: "Stop! That's all I know."

Then Sybilla found her tongue. "But what does it mean, Aunt Maud?"

"It means that messengers have already been sent to the far corners of the duchy. The Duke's vassals will start arriving here soon."

"Papa…"

Her aunt nodded. Bernard de Saint-Valery was the most experienced warrior in the duchy, and the Duke would never go into battle without him. Sybilla went cold all over. As if from a great distance she heard her aunt say: "Your uncle will stay here, of course, but the children and I will return to Barneville. And you, niece, will be going home to Saint-Valery to be with your mother. You won't be safe here, and she will need you."

"Uncle Roger will be staying here?" asked Sybilla.

"Of course," her aunt said impatiently. "Someone has to keep the castle going while the Duke is on the battlefield."

At those words, the reality of the situation hit Sybilla. The English were really coming! If they weren't stopped, Norman soldiers would be killed, castles would be burned, and the countryside would be pillaged. The English soldiers would steal everything edible or valuable, and nobody — peasant, freeman, townsman, priest or lord — would be safe. Her eyes misted over.

"Don't you start," her aunt warned. "There's too much to do. We have to help the Duke prepare for war, and somehow we'll have to get you and your cousins out of here before the English arrive."

"Does Ella know?" she asked, wondering how her other cousin was taking the shocking news.

Her aunt sniffed. "Eleanor has taken to her bed

with a headache. But she won't be there for long, I assure you. I'll need all the help I can get and I expect everyone to pitch in." She gave her son a narrow-eyed look. "And that includes you, Master Raymond."

A week ago, Sybilla's life had been perfectly predictable. She knew that once she had finished her training with the Barnevilles she would marry Geoffrey de Bellême, to whom she had been betrothed since she was a child. But now all these plans were in turmoil. She was elated at the thought of seeing her mother again and returning to her old life on the Saint-Valery estate, but she was worried for her father — and Ella. From what her aunt had said, her cousin seemed to be taking the news of war very hard.

Sybilla ran up the stairs to the Barneville's apartment with Hannibal close behind. As the Duke's right-hand man, her uncle had a suite of rooms reserved for his family's use at the top of the tower. Eleanor was in their room, lying prostrate on the bed the girls shared, a wet cloth over her eyes. Sybilla perched on the side and touched her arm. Eleanor jerked as if she had been burned, then sat up and opened her eyes.

"Oh, Sybilla, thank goodness it's you," she said.

"I thought it was Mama come to drag me out and put me to work." She moaned. "I can't bear it."

One of Eleanor's ears was bright red, and she looked as if she had been crying. Sybilla hugged her cousin, wondering how Eleanor would get on without her when she went home to Saint-Valery. Because they were so close in age — Eleanor was only a year younger — the two had become firm friends. Poor Eleanor had been so lonely before Sybilla had come to the castle. Her father ignored her; Raymond had no interest in his quiet, sensitive sister; and her strong-willed mother bullied her mercilessly, believing she needed toughening up. In Maud's eyes, Eleanor could do no right.

Hannibal put his paws up on the bed and whined in sympathy. "What's wrong, Ella?" asked Sybilla softly. "You're never ill."

Eleanor glanced at Sybilla's concerned face, looking as if she were about to say something, but then changed her mind. "It's nothing."

"Are you frightened, is that it?"

Eleanor hesitated, then said, "Yes, I'm frightened. But I'll get over it." She gave a grim smile. "Mama will see to that."

Sybilla longed to discuss what was going to happen

11

to all of them, but Eleanor's mind seemed to be somewhere else. Slightly hurt, she called Hannibal and made her way to the stables and Dancer's stall. As the stable hand had not yet begun the task, she brushed down her chestnut mare herself. With a great sigh, Hannibal collapsed on a pile of straw and went to sleep, snoring and twitching through his doggy dreams.

Being with Dancer immediately made Sybilla feel calmer. She had inherited her love of horses from her mother, Emma, who had imported Arab and Berber thoroughbreds from Spain and bred them into one of the duchy's most important herds. Almost as soon as she could walk Sybilla had learned to ride, and when Emma had generously offered her a horse of her own, she had chosen the lightest-footed, highest-stepping, most elegant mare on the estate and named her Dancer. Her mother's approving smile had told her she had chosen well.

It wasn't until Sybilla had left home that she realised how much freedom her mother enjoyed. Bernard had no objection to his wife running a horse stud as long as she took her duties as a knight's wife seriously. When Bernard was away fighting for the Duke, Emma ran the estate with the help of her steward, bailiff and reeve. And once, when her husband was in England with the Duke fighting against King William, she had raised a company of freemen and serfs and repelled an armed raid by Gilbert de Montmorency, a distant relative of Bernard who thought he had a claim on Saint-Valery. Sybilla was proud of her independent mother, and her ambition in life was to follow in Emma's footsteps and breed horses.

Aunt Maud was scandalised that a mere girl should own such a valuable animal as Dancer, but Emma had ignored the criticism. "Don't take any notice of Maud," she advised Sybilla. "She's jealous because she's always been too frightened to get on a horse herself. But no daughter of mine will walk or beg for a ride while I own a horse."

Sybilla knew her aunt told anyone who would listen that Sybilla de Saint-Valery was a lazy, spoiled girl. *Perhaps I am spoiled,* she thought. But how could Maud blame Emma for indulging her daughter? Her son Roland was in Burgundy at the court of an ally and her husband was away much of the year fighting the Duke's battles.

That evening, Sybilla's uncle called the family together. As the Duke's steward, Roger de Barneville would be supervising the castle's preparations for war, with the help of the senior courtiers and the Duke's bailiff. But he would also expect his wife, his children and their cousin to do their bit. They gathered together in the adults' bedroom, awaiting his return from a meeting with the Duke.

As soon as his father walked into the room, Raymond leapt up and cried, "What's happening, Papa?" and Maud asked, "Do you know when we shall be leaving here?"

Roger held up an imperious hand to quieten them. "Get me something to eat, Maud. I'm starving. Then I might be able to talk."

Maud went to the door and clapped to summon a servant, who was promptly sent to the kitchen. While he waited for the food, Roger toasted himself in front of the fire; it was always cold in the castle, and winter was just around the corner. When the meal arrived, they tried to contain their impatience while he demolished half a loaf of bread, drained a tankard of ale, and reduced a joint of beef to a bone. This he tossed to Hannibal, who had been sitting with his head on Sybilla's knee, watching Roger with greedy eyes.

Finally Roger wiped his greasy hands on his tunic and turned to Raymond. "Now that Clement has gone home, you can start doing some real work for a change."

Raymond's face fell. His tutor had left the day before to go home to Caen to look after his widowed mother, and he'd been enjoying his freedom. "I want you to stick close to me and do exactly as I say," his father continued. "When I say jump, you'll jump. No disappearing to the guardhouse to gossip. Do you hear me?"

Raymond nodded obediently. Sybilla stifled a grin. Raymond would do exactly as he liked, of course, and his father knew it.

"What about us, Uncle?" asked Sybilla, exchanging glances with Eleanor.

"You two can help Maud. The Duke's knights will start arriving here at first light, and they'll have to be fed and given somewhere to sleep."

As Maud outlined what she expected the girls to do, Sybilla realised that their duties would take them into every part of the castle except the dungeons that housed criminals and enemies of the Duke. They would confer with the cooks in the underground kitchen; visit the castle's gardens to organise vegetables; and relay Maud's orders to the bakery. Sybilla thought it would be much more fun than doing embroidery or learning chess moves. The only drawback was that Aunt Maud was likely to become even more impatient and bad-tempered than usual.

———◦◦◦◦———

As Sybilla and Eleanor lay sleepless in bed that night, Sybilla waited for her cousin to confide in her. Often they laughed and whispered into the night while Hannibal snored at the end of the bed, but tonight Ella was silent. Sybilla was sure she was holding something back. *She'll have to tell me eventually,* she thought. *After all, there's no one else she can talk to.* Turning to look at the tense, silent form beside her, she began to realise how much she was going to miss Eleanor. She'd never minded having no sisters because she didn't know what she was missing, but she had grown to love her gentle cousin, and leaving her would be a terrible wrench.

Chapter Two

Sybilla and Eleanor rose at dawn the next day and took up their duties. The castle grounds were mad with dust and din. Carpenters were hard at work fashioning bows and arrows out of wood and cowhide, and a blast of heat and smoke and the deafening clang of metal on anvil emanated from a workshop where brawny, muscular blacksmiths beat molten iron into horseshoes, shields and spears. Artisans fashioned chain mail for the knights to deflect the axes and swords of their enemies. Stonemasons examined the castle walls, looking for weaknesses and making repairs. The grooms and stable hands reshoed the Duke's warhorses, and leatherworkers repaired saddles.

As she passed through the castle forecourt, Sybilla reflected that the threat of war had brought people together. Old squabbles and slights were forgotten, and knights worked alongside serfs and freemen in a common cause.

For most of the day, Sybilla was kept too busy to fret, but the moment she stopped to eat, her mind turned to her father. She was worried. Bernard de Saint-Valery was a celebrated warrior and had survived many battles before now, but from what she had heard of King William, Sybilla knew he would be a dangerous foe. And although she was anxious for her father to arrive at the castle, she knew their time together would be short, and the parting painful.

———≈○●○≈———

Early that afternoon, one of the watchmen sent a messenger to Sybilla, who was helping peel what felt like thousands of turnips in the kitchen. When she learned that her father was approaching the castle, she dropped what she was doing and rushed up to the battlements to look. At first she thought she'd been misled — all she could see was a line of carts making its way towards the drawbridge. But there — behind a wagon loaded high with bales of wool bound for the castle spinning room — what was that? A small group of horsemen flying the Saint-Valery standard! At its head was a giant of a man with blond hair and a ginger beard. Sybilla's heart pounded, and she ran down to meet him in the cobbled courtyard.

"Papa, Papa!" she shouted.

Bernard's face lit up when he caught sight of his daughter, and he leapt off his horse to embrace her. Enveloped in his bear hug, Sybilla felt safe for the first time since she had heard about the impending war. She inhaled her father's familiar smell of horse, leather and hay, and laughed when his beard tickled her face. Then Bernard's stallion snorted, reminding them where they were. Sybilla had a hundred questions, but they would have to wait until her father had paid his respects to the Duke.

Sybilla returned to her tasks, but time passed slowly as she waited impatiently for her father's summons. Finally, a messenger appeared to tell Sybilla that Bernard wanted to see her. He was waiting in the armoury.

Sybilla ran to the armoury, where she found her father and uncle in a corner with their heads together. She had never entered this grand room before, and gazed around in awe. It was here that the Duke's vassals came to pay him homage, and where he received ambassadors from other royal courts. The walls of the armoury were adorned with weapons and suits of armour. But they weren't just decorations; all of them had been worn by soldiers in battle. *How many of them never came back?* she wondered.

Seeing her hovering at the door, her father called out to her. She went and stood beside his chair, and he put an arm around her waist. "Do you know Odo du Vast, the Duke's secretary?" he asked.

Sybilla had seen Odo around the castle, but he had never deigned to speak to her. He was very proud of his position, and was known to kick and strike servants who did not jump to attention when he shouted. Most people gave him a wide berth.

"Yes I do, Papa," she said cautiously. "Why?"

"He has agreed to escort you home."

Sybilla must have flinched, for her father said, "We must be grateful to the Duke for sparing him." He gave her a squeeze. "Odo will look after you. He knows how valuable you are to me. And how valuable I am to the Duke."

"I know Odo has a temper on him, niece," said her uncle, "but he's strong and can wield a sword."

Sybilla hoped so. Saint-Valery was a long way from Rouen, and who knew what dangers lay in wait along the road? She had heard stories about bandits robbing farmers on market day and leaving them with nothing but the clothes they stood up in. And there were dark tales of beatings and even deaths when their victims resisted.

Her father read her mind. "If you leave at dawn, you will be home safe by midnight. Don't be afraid, daughter. There will be travellers on the roads. If anything happens, they'll help you."

"Yes, Papa," she said dutifully. Her father had enough on his mind without having to worry about her. "I'm sure I'll be all right."

Her uncle was growing restless. "Run along now," he said. "Your father and I have important matters to discuss."

Later that day Raymond sneaked into the kitchen to tell Sybilla that Robert de Bellême and his men were approaching the castle. Sybilla dropped her paring knife in shock. It hadn't occurred to her that her fiancé, Geoffrey de Bellême, would be joining the Duke's army. She still thought of him as the boy she'd met two years before, but of course he was old enough to fight now. Ella, who had been cutting apples into slices for a pie, had never seen Geoffrey and was curious. "Let's go and look, Sybilla," she urged.

Sybilla nodded shyly, and the cousins took off their aprons and ran up to the battlements. By this time, the Bellême party was clattering across the drawbridge. "There he is, Ella," she said, pointing to a slim, dark-haired young man on a black steed.

"He's gorgeous," said Eleanor with a giggle. "Is he rich, too?"

Sybilla laughed. "Of course. He's the heir to the Bellême estate, which is huge. My mother would never let me marry a poor man and become a drudge."

"But she married a poor man herself," argued Eleanor.

"Mama was lucky — she had her own fortune. But I shall have to marry well or be poor, because Roland will inherit Saint-Valery." Sybilla sent up a little prayer of thanks that Roland was a squire in the court of Count Robert of Burgundy, and would not be joining the Duke's army. "Thank God he's safe. It would be too terrible for Mama to…" She could not finish the thought.

Kind-hearted Eleanor put out her hand and stroked Sybilla's arm. She knew what her cousin meant: if both her husband and son died on the battlefield, not only would Emma de Saint-Valery have the grief to bear; she would also be in a difficult political position. She would either have to marry again, or try to run the estate alone and without protection. Eleanor changed the subject. "What is Geoffrey like, cousin?"

Sybilla shrugged. "I've only met him once, when we were betrothed. He seemed amiable enough, but all he could talk about was fighting. I suppose you can't blame him — he's been training to be a soldier his whole life, practically." She frowned. "We really didn't have anything in common except our love of horses." But she thought he would make a decent enough husband, which was the best she could hope for. This was not to be a love match; she understood that their marriage was about property and political power. They had been pledged to each other because their parents owned adjoining estates — though the Bellême estate was much bigger — and both families owed fealty to Robert of Normandy.

When Sybilla thought about marrying Geoffrey, it was not romance she imagined; rather, she worried about how she would fit into such a grand family and how her future mother-in-law, Blanche de Bellême, would treat her. Blanche was a formidable and proud woman, and Sybilla had no doubt that she would expect her daughter-in-law to conduct herself in a manner befitting a grand lady. And Blanche would almost certainly oppose her plan to breed horses. She was not looking forward to the battle of wills, and hoped fervently that Geoffrey would take his part.

Knowing Geoffrey de Bellême was in the castle made Sybilla jumpy, and she worried as she went about her tasks. Would he want to see her? Did she want to see him? She wasn't sure. At last Aunt Maud found her in the bakery counting loaves of bread, and announced that Geoffrey had indeed asked to see her. Her aunt bade Sybilla return to their quarters and dress herself appropriately.

Sybilla rushed off obediently, her mind in a whirl, but whether her jitters came from fear or excitement she hardly knew. When Eleanor entered the room a few minutes later, she found her cousin surrounded by clothes. Sybilla, who would have been happier in boys' breeches, seized Eleanor by the hand gratefully. "I'm so glad you're here, Ella. Tell me what to wear."

Eleanor rummaged through the pile of garments and pulled out a cornflower blue tunic. "You have to wear this. It shows off your complexion. And put this lovely mantle over it."

She held up the mantle, which was richly embroidered in blue and gold, and seemed to glow in the light. Sybilla cherished it because Roland had sent it from Burgundy for her last birthday. Sybilla donned a plain linen tunic, pulled the blue tunic over it, and wound the mantle over her shoulders and tried to tug it into place. Eleanor clucked her tongue and rearranged the robe artistically, fastening it at the neck with a brooch she took from her own outfit. "There, you see. Now, let's find a veil."

Another search through the pile of clothing unearthed a blue veil that matched Sybilla's tunic perfectly. Eleanor stood back, surveying her cousin critically as she adjusted the veil to cover her head and shoulders, leaving only her face visible. Then she sorted through Sybilla's jewellery chest and selected some pieces. First she placed a gold band on Sybilla's head to hold the veil in place. "What a pity you have to cover up your beautiful golden hair," she remarked.

Sybilla flushed. She was inordinately proud of her long blonde plait, and had more than once had to do penance for the sin of vanity.

Finally, Eleanor slipped onto Sybilla's wrists the two gold bracelets she had inherited from her grandmother. "Now you're ready."

Sybilla examined herself in the looking glass. She barely recognised the fashionable young woman staring back at her. If her father passed her in the corridor, he would probably not know her.

———◦◦◦———

Geoffrey was already waiting when Sybilla arrived in her aunt's room, looking as nervous as she felt. He rose and bowed when she entered — and blushed deeply. Aunt Maud, who was acting as chaperone, was seated nearby, watching their every move. Sybilla stole a glance at Geoffrey, then lowered her eyes modestly, aware of her aunt's eyes on her.

The conversation limped along awkwardly. Geoffrey told Sybilla that he intended to return to Bellême after the war and learn how to run the estate. *If he survives,* she thought. Sybilla, in turn, talked about her life in the castle, describing the parade of lords and ladies who came to pay homage to the Duke, and the grand banquets that were held for foreign ambassadors and princes.

It was only when Geoffrey asked about her animals that she began to warm to him. "Dancer is learning to jump hurdles, milord. Hannibal's nose is as keen as ever, although he has not had much opportunity to hunt lately. And Merlin is now fully trained."

As she spoke, Sybilla finally dared to look directly at Geoffrey, and found him staring back, his keen brown eyes fixed on her face. In the two years since she had seen him, he had grown taller and more handsome. His features seemed finer, and his hair, which he wore long, was thick and lustrous.

With Aunt Maud hovering over them, the two young people quickly ran out of things to talk about. When they subsided into embarrassed silence, Maud cleared her throat to signal the end of the visit. Geoffrey took the hint, and rose to go. But before he left, he handed Sybilla a tiny carved wooden casket. She opened it to find a little gold ring set with a glowing red stone. "It's beautiful," she whispered.

"It's a memento, milady." His voice faltered. "Something to remind you of me."

Sybilla quavered her thanks, and bobbed a curtsy before rushing from the room. It didn't seem fair! Just as she was beginning to get to know Geoffrey — and like him — he had to go off to war. Back in the room she shared with Ella, she examined the ring more closely. Her eyes filled with tears when she saw *Geoffrey & Sybilla forever* engraved inside it.

Sybilla was in the kitchen later that day when a servant rushed in to tell the cook the latest news. The King of England had landed on the coast of Normandy! *It was really happening!* Sybilla realised. The blood drained from her heart, and she dropped the bowl she was holding, watching it fall, ever so slowly, before it smashed to smithereens on the stone floor.

———————————

That night Sybilla had her last dinner in the Great Hall. She dressed carefully and joined her aunt and Eleanor at one of the long tables; as usual, Raymond was off on some intrigue of his own. Her father and uncle, as the Duke's steward and Normandy's most valiant knight, would sit at the head table with the Duke. The hall was even more crowded than usual, as all the duchy's knights had now gathered at the castle to join the Duke's army. Sybilla looked around and found Geoffrey seated on the other side of the room with his father and some lords she did not know. He caught her eye and inclined his head, making her blush furiously. Eleanor noticed, and nudged her with her elbow.

"It's not like you to blush over a man, cousin,"

said Eleanor in a teasing tone. "Don't tell me you've fallen in love."

"I hardly know him!" protested Sybilla. The last thing she wanted was to be in love with someone who was going off to war. It was bad enough that she had to worry about her father.

Eleanor was about to say something else, when Aunt Maud intervened. "Behave yourselves, you two!" she snapped.

The girls ceased their chatter, and Sybilla retreated into her own thoughts. Now that her stay in Rouen was almost over, she realised how lucky she had been to live in such opulent surroundings with such important people. She surveyed the Great Hall as if seeing it for the first time. It was very grand, with heavy carved beams overhead, and huge carved sideboards loaded with gold and pewter platters and ewers. The flag of Normandy and other banners and pennants hung from the walls, which were decorated with shields, crossed lances and battleaxes. At one end of the hall was a fireplace big enough to burn whole logs; tonight the fire was blazing, sending out a blast of heat and a cloud of smoke. The din was tremendous.

But suddenly a hush fell, and all eyes turned to

the entrance. The Duke had arrived. Followed by his favourite courtiers and most trusted knights, Robert of Normandy advanced to the front of the room. Just before he took his place on the high table, Raymond darted in, earning a cuff on the ear from his mother. When they were seated and the Duke had called for food, the noise started up again. Servants rushed in carrying huge platters of meat and vegetables; others brought flagons of wine and jugs of ale. Then the minstrels began to play and sing for the company.

Everyone tried to be festive and laugh at the jester's jokes, but the imminence of war cast a pall of fear and gloom over the gathering. Aunt Maud felt it and took early leave from the banquet with her family. The women curtsied, Raymond bowed to the Duke, and Sybilla stole one last look at Geoffrey to find that, once again, he was watching her.

Knowing that the army would be setting out the following morning, Sybilla found it hard to sleep that night. Next to her in the big bed Eleanor tossed and turned too.

Something awoke Sybilla at dawn, and she opened her eyes to find her father sitting on the side of her bed staring down at her. He looked sad.

"Papa, what's wrong?" she asked.

Bernard put his big hand on Sybilla's shoulder to soothe her. "I wanted a moment with you before all the madness starts," he said. "I have something for you from your mother." He reached into a pocket and pulled out a necklet made of cloth with a little pouch on the end. Sybilla caught her breath. It was the relic her grandfather had brought home from his pilgrimage to Jerusalem!

"But Mama never takes this off!" she said, reaching out to touch it.

Bernard looped the pendant over Sybilla's head and smoothed it down. Her hand immediately flew up to caress the holy pebble inside the pouch.

"It's for you to wear home, Sybilla. It has protected Emma all these years, and she wants you to be safe on your journey."

"Oh, Papa," she wailed. Eleanor mumbled something in her sleep and, not wanting to wake her, they fell silent for a moment. When Ella began to breathe deeply again, Bernard embraced his daughter. "Don't cry, Sybilla. It's going to be hard enough for me to leave here without worrying about you. Be brave for me."

Sybilla hiccoughed and nodded into his chest. When she had recovered, Bernard stood up. "Wear your prettiest dress today. I want to see my beautiful girl smiling and waving me goodbye when I set off."

Sybilla mentally finished the sentence for him: *Because it might be the last time we ever see each other.*

CHAPTER THREE

The next morning saw all the castle's inhabitants gathered for a solemn ceremony in the chapel. Lit only by a few flickering candles the chapel was gloomy — and chilly. But the atmosphere seemed right for such a sombre occasion. Sybilla gazed at the ornately carved depiction of the crucifixion over the altar and at the tombs of the Duke's ancestors buried in the thick walls; this would be the last time she would pray here.

She had spent many hours on her knees in this church asking for forgiveness for disobeying her aunt, or daydreaming when she should have been sewing, or being angry and resentful when she was criticised or punished. But it was a sacred and peaceful place, and despite its simplicity it always filled her with a sense of awe. As Sybilla watched the Bishop of Rouen bless her father and her future husband, and joined in the prayers for their victory, she thought her heart would burst with pride for her valiant knights. But her elation was mixed with sadness, too, for the hour of departure had finally arrived.

Sybilla joined the Barneville family at the castle gates to watch the Norman forces march off to war. The trumpets sounded and colourful flags billowed in the wind. Leading the parade was the Duke. Although he was short and quite stout, Robert looked every inch a warrior prince today, astride his black warhorse. He was flanked by his most trusted and courageous knights, one of whom was Bernard de Saint-Valery. Sybilla saw her father scanning the crowd, and waved to him. He finally caught sight of her and saluted. And there was Geoffrey, riding beside his father, Robert de Bellême.

The Duke's army was impressive. The knights wore conical steel helmets on top of woven metal hoods, and thigh-length chain mail shirts over padded jerkins. Each carried a wooden shield in one hand and a lance and a heavy, blunt-tipped sword in the other. A few carried longbows and others simple crossbows. Marching in tight formation behind the knights and the cavalry were the foot soldiers.

The small crowd cheered and waved, but Sybilla couldn't bring herself to join in. Then a soft hand stole into hers, and she turned to see Eleanor gazing at her, her hazel eyes filled with sympathy. "I'm sure God will spare your father, Sybilla," she whispered. "And Geoffrey. They are both good men."

Sybilla squeezed Eleanor's hand, and wished she had her cousin's faith. In her years at the castle in Rouen, she had seen several good men come to grief at the hands of their fellow countrymen. What chance would they have at the hands of the bloodthirsty English? The crowd cheered itself hoarse until the column of soldiers disappeared into the distance, then quietly dispersed. The girls went inside, weary from the frantic activity of the last two days and wrung-out from loss. Even Maud de Barneville was exhausted from the effort of preparing for war, and promptly retired to her room. Her husband disappeared to confer with the Duke's other officials.

After all the bustle, the girls finally found themselves without anything to do. "Let's go up to the battlements," Eleanor suggested. "We'll be able to see the soldiers a bit longer from there."

It was still early, and a brisk wind swept through their vantage point. And there in the distance they could see the Norman forces snaking their way up a hill. Once they had crested the rise, they would be gone.

Sybilla shivered, and was about to suggest they descend when her cousin put her hand on her arm.

"Sybilla," said Eleanor tentatively, "I want to tell you something."

"What is it, Ella?" Sybilla asked absently, still straining her eyes in the hope of catching one last glimpse of her father or Geoffrey in the column of men.

"I've done something terrible."

Surprised, Sybilla turned. When she saw Eleanor's grave face and huge, tear-filled eyes, her heart skipped a beat. "What are you talking about, Ella? You've never done a bad thing in your life. I sometimes wonder what on earth you can find to tell the priest when you go to confession."

"I've fallen in love with Clement."

Sybilla's eyes widened in disbelief at what she was hearing. Eleanor was a lady whose father was an intimate of a duke, and Clement was only a tutor. They could never marry. Besides, Eleanor was already betrothed. "But Ella, you've been promised to Alan Peverel since you were seven!"

"Alan is a bore," Eleanor flashed. "All he can talk

about is those pigs he breeds! At least Clement is interesting."

It was true that Clement was a man of many talents. He was highly educated, widely travelled and spoke several languages, and had often enthralled them with his tales of the exotic people and places he had visited. "And he loves me," said Eleanor defiantly.

Sybilla was dumbstruck. Had her cousin and the tutor been carrying out a clandestine courtship all this time? But although she racked her brains, she could not recall anything suspicious, any secret messages or signals passing between them. "Did he say something to you, Ella?"

"Just before he left, he caught me alone. He was all tongue-tied, and I knew he wanted to tell me something, but he didn't dare. So I told him I loved him." She laughed. "I thought he'd faint from shock."

At her cousin's utter astonishment, Eleanor looked stubborn. "I've adored him from the moment I saw him, Sybilla. I know my own heart."

Sybilla regarded her quiet cousin with a new respect, and wondered if she had ever really known her. "It's all so surprising, Ella. You're usually so good and well-behaved."

"I'm not really," protested Eleanor. "It's just that I've learned to hold my tongue." She gave her cousin a sidelong look. "Like you have." Eleanor smiled at Sybilla's guilty flush. "Mama taught me that by slapping me every time I opened my mouth."

"I just can't understand how you didn't give yourself away," said Sybilla.

Eleanor smiled. "Oh, Clement knew right from the start. You can feel these things."

If she hadn't felt so frightened for her cousin, Sybilla could almost have envied her certainty. She couldn't decide what she felt about Geoffrey after yesterday's meeting. She'd barely given him a thought in the last few years, whereas now… She thought about the little ruby ring, with its secret inscription. "But you know nothing can come of it, don't you, Ella? Your mother…"

Eleanor shuddered. "If she ever finds out, she'll lock me up until my wedding day."

"What are you going to do?"

"I don't know," said Eleanor helplessly. "But I *will* marry Clement."

I've underestimated her all this time, thought Sybilla, amazed. *And I thought I knew everything about her.* She wondered how many people led secret lives. She'd always thought it would be impossible to have a secret with Raymond around… Which reminded her: she had not seen Raymond for hours. "Eleanor, where is Raymond?" she asked sharply.

Eleanor shrugged. "I imagine he's around somewhere. I can never keep up with his comings and goings."

Sybilla pinched her cousin on the arm. "Wake up, Ella. When did you see him last?"

"Ouch!" said her cousin indignantly, rubbing her arm. "This morning, at breakfast."

The girls gazed at one another in horror as the awful truth dawned. "He's gone with the Duke!" cried Eleanor in dismay. "What should we do?"

What indeed? If they told Raymond's parents, a search party would be organised to bring him back and Raymond would never forgive them. If they didn't tell, and the Barnevilles found out that they had known, the girls' lives would not be worth living. As they stood there in an agony of indecision, they heard shouting below. Then the gates flew open and Roger de Barneville and two of his servants erupted from the castle and galloped after the army.

The girls watched the men until they disappeared, then turned and looked at each other and burst out laughing. Then Eleanor became serious. "I'm going to miss you, Sybilla," she said. "If you hadn't been here, my life would have been intolerable."

"I never really did anything to help you against your mother," said Sybilla remorsefully.

Eleanor reached out and touched her hand. "Yes, you did. You tried to stand up for me. You only stopped because you realised it made Mama worse. But I knew how you felt, and it gave me strength."

Sybilla did not see Raymond again that day. He was hustled into the castle in disgrace and locked up in the dungeon until the army was too far away for him to reach. She spent the day preparing for her journey, packing her clothing into saddlebags and her jewellery into a pouch to wear close to her skin. The Barnevilles were about to leave, too. Maud rushed about barking orders at servants and at Eleanor. Until a few days ago her mother's bullying would have reduced Eleanor to tears, but now she seemed impervious. Sybilla suspected she was dreaming of Clement.

As they would be leaving at dawn, everybody went to bed early. Excited about seeing her mother again, worried about the journey, and starting to miss Eleanor and Raymond already, Sybilla slept badly. Hannibal, who had the uncanny knack of picking up her moods, leapt onto the bed with her and licked her face. Usually this made Sybilla laugh, but tonight it didn't work.

CHAPTER FOUR

Sybilla woke before daybreak and sat up, waking Hannibal. He gave a surprised bark that woke Eleanor. When they had dressed, they looked at each other sorrowfully.

"You've been like a sister to me, Ella," said Sybilla.

Hannibal, who had a kind heart, came up and thrust his big head between them. Eleanor absently pulled his long ears, but when he slobbered on her, pushed him away gently. "I know. I'm dreading going home without you. How am I going to survive alone with Mama?"

"I'll pray for you," promised Sybilla.

"And I'll pray that we win the war, and that our men come home safely. And that you get home in one piece. I just wish I were going with you."

"Wake up, sleepyheads," said a voice from the doorway. It was Raymond.

"Raymond! They've let you out!" cried Sybilla.

"Not quite. I escaped."

Sybilla and Eleanor laughed. Raymond had made it his business to befriend every soldier and guard in the castle, and his foresight had obviously paid off. "I didn't want you to leave without saying goodbye."

"We didn't tell on you, Raymond…" said his sister.

"I know. Mama missed me and got suspicious." He rubbed his buttocks ruefully. "She gave me a good whipping when Papa brought me back." He grinned. "But it was worth it. Another couple of hours and I would have got away with it."

"I'm glad you didn't," said Sybilla firmly. "We've all got enough to worry about already. Anyway," she sighed, "I suppose I should get a move on. I don't want Odo to have to come looking for me. Imagine what kind of mood *that* would put him in!"

"I wish you weren't going with that man," said Raymond. "I don't trust him."

"Don't say that, Raymond. I'm frightened enough already. And besides, I have no choice."

They were interrupted by the sound of Maud de Barneville in full flight. "Raymond! Where is that boy? Don't tell me he's run away again!"

"I'd better go," said Raymond, slipping through the door. "I'll see you girls at breakfast."

The whole family was subdued at breakfast, conscious that this was their last meal together. And who knew when they would all meet again? After they had eaten, Aunt Maud had the maid fetch Sybilla a small hamper of food — bread, cheese, ale, a chicken leg, apples and water, and some bones for Hannibal — and kissed her niece. As she accepted the parcel, Sybilla felt a little guilty about all the unkind thoughts she'd had about her aunt. Maud couldn't help her nature, and she could be generous and caring. What a pity they had never become friends.

But it was too late now for regrets. Sybilla took leave of her uncle and aunt, and the cousins made their way to the falconry, where Sybilla placed Merlin carefully in his wooden travelling box. Then they proceeded to the stables, Raymond carrying Sybilla's saddlebags, Sybilla carrying Merlin in his box and Eleanor following with Hannibal.

Dawn was approaching, and the castle was beginning to stir. A few sleepy servants were emerging, yawning and scratching themselves, to wash their faces under the pumps. Smoke billowed from the castle kitchens. The bakers had been up for hours already, and the tantalising aroma of fresh bread wafted from the bakery. As Sybilla saddled

Dancer and Raymond slung the saddlebags over the horse's belly and did up the buckles, the mare began to prance, excited at the prospect of a journey. Hannibal caught her mood and began to bark. Sybilla ordered her bloodhound to hush, mounted and placed the hawk box in front of her.

Odo arrived soon after, looking grumpy and dishevelled. A well-built man in his thirties, he would have been good-looking but for his perpetually aggrieved expression. He grunted a greeting, and shouted at the groom to get a move on. The groom, cringing as if he expected a blow, obeyed and Odo swung himself up on to his horse. It was time to go. Hannibal ran back for one last lick of Raymond's face, and Sybilla craned back for another glimpse of her cousins. They waved, and she tried to smile at them reassuringly.

Then Sybilla and her surly escort passed through the castle gates, and were on the road. Narrow and rutted from the carts that brought provisions to the castle, the road was dusty now from the drought that had brought misery to Normandy over the last year. It was so early that an occasional owl ghosted past on its way home from hunting. A chorus of birds greeted the sunrise, and soon after smoke began to rise from the chimneys of the thatched cottages they passed, and cocks began to crow across the countryside.

People began to appear on the road, some walking, others riding in donkey carts, sometimes with wives and children. In good times these carts would be loaded with produce for the markets, but today they often held only a few ears of corn, some withered apples, woody-looking turnips, and occasionally a wheel of hard cheese. Later a herdsman held them up while his goats crossed the road, leaving their pungent smell hanging on the morning air.

As they ventured deeper into the countryside, Sybilla saw first-hand the effects of the long drought. They had scarcely felt it in the castle, but the chaplain had asked them all to pray for rain to alleviate the suffering of the peasants. From what Sybilla had seen since she left Rouen, it seemed that God had not yet answered their prayers. Instead of fields of rye and corn, the crops were stunted and scorched looking. Vegetable patches lay empty. What cows and sheep remained were thin and bony. Even the grass along the road verges was dry and brittle.

As the day grew warmer, Sybilla removed her cloak and began to enjoy the feel of the sun on her face and the wonderful freedom that travel brings, that sense of being suspended between two worlds and having no responsibilities. Odo's stubborn silence was a godsend, as it let her think in peace. Whenever she or Eleanor had dared to daydream at the castle, Aunt Maud would immediately find a chore for them to do. "The devil finds work for idle hands," she would scold, shooing the girls ahead of her like a farmer's wife sweeping hens out of her way. The memory made Sybilla chuckle, and Odo shot her a suspicious glance.

When the sun reached its zenith, Odo called a halt and they ate lunch under an oak tree so old it must have sheltered hundreds of generations of birds. Sybilla watered and fed Dancer and Hannibal, who had heroically kept up with the horses, and let Merlin loose before tucking into bread and cheese and a draught of ale. The sun's rays were soporific, and soon Dancer's head drooped and Hannibal began to snore loudly. Half-asleep herself, Sybilla was jolted awake by the sound of horses' hooves on the road. She sat up and watched as two riders approached. One was a young gentleman and the other may have been his servant. Were they friend or foe? Whoever they were, she had never seen them before. Sybilla looked to Odo to see how he would respond, but he simply ignored the men. Sybilla thought that slightly odd, but Odo's moods were unpredictable. But when the riders moved on without incident, she relaxed once more.

Shortly after, Odo leapt to his feet and announced that it was time to go. Hannibal woke and shook his great jowls to clear his head, spraying drool far and wide. Dancer snorted and stamped as Sybilla called Merlin down from an oak tree and returned him to his box, and they started out again. As Sybilla's father had predicted, there had been a constant stream of traffic on the road, and Sybilla had started to wonder why she had been so apprehensive about this journey.

But her confidence was replaced by a sense of foreboding when they came to a wood. If there were bandits in the area, this was surely where they would lie in wait for unwary travellers. Her pulse quickened. She glanced over at Odo and noticed that his hand had fallen to his sword. That was a good sign: at least he was on the alert and prepared to defend them.

The deeper they went into the woods, the gloomier it grew. The trees were so dense that sound became strangely muffled. At one point Sybilla was sure she heard a horse whinny softly, and Hannibal pricked up his ears, stopped, and looked around. And then it happened. As they turned a bend in the road they found themselves face to face with two masked horsemen, who blocked their way menacingly. Dancer reared up in shock, and Sybilla struggled to cling on as the saddlebags were flung back against her legs. With one hand gripping Dancer's mane, she reached desperately for Merlin's box as it teetered and fell from the horse. She cried out in dismay as it hit the ground and sprang open. The impact loosened the bird's tether and he flew away. To Sybilla's relief, he seemed unhurt.

But then the men drew their swords, and she forgot about Merlin. Her heart thudding, Sybilla turned to Odo for help and saw, with a lurch of fear in her stomach, that he was no longer by her side. He must have fled while she was distracted by Dancer! Where had he gone? Surely he wouldn't desert her?

"Just stay calm, milady, and nothing bad will happen to you," growled one of the bandits. He was a slender young man with a cultured accent that did not match his clothes — in fact, he sounded like a gentleman.

And he called me "milady", thought Sybilla. *Does he know who I am? Or is it my clothing that gives me away?* "Who are you? What do you want?" she asked, trying to keep her voice even and calm.

"Your jewellery, for a start," said the second man. He was small and skinny with bad teeth and pockmarks on his exposed neck. It was then that Sybilla recognised them: they were the horsemen who had overtaken her and Odo on the road earlier. The pockmarked thief rode up beside her, pointed his sword at her heart, and put out his hand with an evil grin. Knowing a villain when she smelled one, Dancer shied, and Sybilla had to dig her heels in to bring the mare under control.

"Get a move on," ordered the bandit. "Or do I have to search you?"

Sybilla flushed scarlet with rage and humiliation. If only she had a weapon of her own… But it was no use being foolish. A little hoard of gold and coloured stones was not worth dying for. *But they're not getting my dog,* she thought, as she noticed the man eyeing her well-bred bloodhound appreciatively. Merlin had left of his own accord, but she knew Hannibal would never desert his post. She would have to force him to leave.

"Go, Hannibal!" she shouted, glaring at the dog and clapping her hands angrily. Hannibal whined and dropped his head and tail; abandoning his mistress alone went against all his instincts and training. Sybilla almost gave up, but she had to remain firm for both of them. "Bad dog!" she cried. "I told you to go!" Finally the hound turned and loped off into the trees. He stopped and looked back, but when Sybilla pointed imperiously, he bounded off.

Strengthened by the knowledge that at least Hannibal was safe, Sybilla reached under her mantle, undid her jewellery pouch and handed it over. The pockmarked bandit ripped it open and pawed through her trinkets greedily. She was glad she had hung Geoffrey's little ring on a ribbon around her neck and tucked it out of sight under her tunic. The very thought of strangers handling her token made her blood run cold.

By this time she was recovering from the initial shock, and was determined to get away. Surely they would see no need to pursue her now that they had her valuables. She dug her heels into Dancer's flanks and shouted, "Giddyap!" The chestnut mare reared up, ready to flee, but the skinny thief was too fast for her. He grabbed the reins and held tight until Dancer stilled. Then he ordered Sybilla to dismount. When she hesitated, he shouted, "I said, get down!"

Trembling, she jumped down from the horse, and watched helplessly as he slapped Dancer heavily on the rump and yelled, "Git!" Dancer, who had never before been struck in anger, neighed and galloped away.

Watching her horse disappear down the road, Sybilla felt lonelier than she ever had in her life. Lowering her eyes, she stole a glance into the undergrowth, trying to catch a glimpse of Hannibal. There was no sign of movement.

The pockmarked man's voice interrupted her thoughts: "You're riding with me." When Sybilla did not move quickly enough, he said: "Are you deaf, missy? Get up here, now!" He put his hand down, and she grasped his arm and swung herself on the back of his horse.

"Cover her eyes," said the cultured young man. The pockmarked thief handed her a dirty kerchief and ordered her to put it on. Sybilla obeyed, but was careful not to tie it too tightly. Then he barked, "Let's go!", and they thundered off in the direction of Saint-Valery. Did they know where she lived? Perhaps they were planning to deposit her somewhere near her home?

But Sybilla soon discovered that they were not taking her home. A couple of leagues past the woods, they stopped, then turned off to the right. Sybilla deduced that they had reached a crossroads and turned north. That meant they were heading for Flanders, the county ruled by the Duke's cousin. As they travelled farther and farther from everything Sybilla knew, she allowed herself to hope that Odo had not abandoned her, and had instead returned to Rouen for help. But in her heart she knew he had betrayed her — though why, and to whom, she had no idea. What on earth could her captors want with her? She only knew one thing for sure as the motion of the horse lulled her into an uncomfortable doze: she was on her own.

Chapter Five

Sybilla jerked awake suddenly to find her nose pressed against her abductor's smelly jerkin. The horse had come to a halt. But where were they, and why were the thieves stopping? The pockmarked thief dismounted and began muttering to the young gentleman. Feeling terribly vulnerable without the use of her eyes, Sybilla strained her ears, but could not make out what they were saying.

Then her abductor ordered her to get down, holding her arm tightly in case she fell or decided to run. When she regained her balance, he said, "This way," and dragged her into some sort of building.

The ground was soft under foot; there was either hay or rushes on the floor. Then Sybilla smelled horse and chicken manure. She must be in a barn. Which meant there must be a farmhouse nearby. And people. Then she was roughly shoved and fell over. She flailed her arms and let out a shout, afraid she would be hurt, but she landed in a pile of straw.

When she tried to get up, her captor held her down. "Don't move!" he ordered. Then he walked away and she heard him outside, talking to the young gentleman. What were they planning? A horse whinnied and one of the thieves galloped away. It turned out to be the thief with pockmarks, for when someone appeared at her side moments later, said "Have some water," and placed an earthenware flask into her hands, she recognised the gentleman's voice.

"It will be easier for me to drink if you take my blindfold off," said Sybilla.

The man laughed, not unkindly. "Nice try, milady. But you don't need your eyes to drink." He paused. "Or don't you want it?" He started to pull the flask out of her grasp, but Sybilla, who was parched, hung on tight. The kidnapper chuckled and let go. "I thought so."

She drank a long draught of water and immediately felt better. The thief took the bottle from her and went outside, no doubt to stand watch. For a while Sybilla tried to stay alert and listen for clues as to her fate, but as time passed and nothing happened, she became despondent and listless. She was startled back to awareness by a sharp peck on her hand. She suppressed a little shriek and sat up. Then her attacker snuggled its head under her chin and chirped. "Merlin," she whispered, and smoothed down the little falcon's feathers.

The serious falconers at the castle had warned her that she was making Merlin too tame by spoiling him, that becoming too close to humans would ruin him as a hunter, but Sybilla had resisted treating her bird harshly. Now she was glad she had not. At least she wasn't completely alone. But where on earth was poor Hannibal? Eventually the light filtering through Sybilla's blindfold dimmed, and she guessed that twilight had fallen. There was no sign of the young gentleman, and his accomplice had not returned.

Galvanised by Merlin's reappearance, Sybilla bucked up and tried to analyse her predicament. If her captors intended to harm her, wouldn't they have done so already? And if they'd only wanted her jewellery, why hadn't they taken it and fled? They must have other plans. If they wanted her alive and well, they must be holding her hostage, she concluded. If so, the pockmarked man might have gone to the castle to negotiate the ransom with her uncle… But surely he wouldn't dare enter the heavily fortified castle; her uncle would throw him into the dungeon.

So he must be on his way to Saint-Valery to talk terms with her mother. *How much ransom money would her abductors demand?* the girl wondered. What did they believe she was worth to Emma? Her mother would find it difficult to raise a large sum, but the kidnappers did not know this. Her parents poured all their money into the estate, and never had large amounts of cash or gold at their disposal. Really, the only thing of value her family owned was the estate itself.

Sybilla began to worry in earnest now. What would happen to her if her mother could not pay the ransom? Would they demand the deeds of the estate instead? The thought filled Sybilla with dread. Imagine if her father came home from war to discover that Saint-Valery had been lost in his absence! Or if not the estate, Sybilla herself… For a moment she felt hopeless, but then her temper came to her rescue. Instead of sitting here waiting for a rescue that might never come, she must try to escape.

After listening quietly for a few minutes, and deciding that her abductor was not nearby, she took off her blindfold and looked around. She'd been right: it was a barn. She had hoped that the barn would be close to a farmhouse, with people who might help her, but it looked disused and neglected. Boards were missing from the walls, but the gaps didn't look wide enough for her to squeeze through. She grabbed one of the poles that supported the hayloft above her to pull herself to her feet — and was shocked into stillness when it moved. Afraid the loft would collapse and fall on her, she let go immediately.

Then she paused and thought. Dare she try it? Would it work? After surveying the barn, the rickety hayloft, the distance to the door and the light, she decided it just might. Replacing her blindfold, she called out: "Help! Oh, please help me! I'm ill!"

Her cries alarmed Merlin, who fluttered upwards and found a perch high on the barn wall. They must have frightened the bandit, too, for he came rushing into the barn looking dishevelled, as if he'd been asleep. "What's wrong, milady?" he asked. He seemed worried. Of course he would be, Sybilla reasoned. If something happened to their hostage, the kidnappers might not get their money, and he would be blamed.

"I've got an awful stomach ache," she gasped. "Please, could you get me a drink of water?"

The young man rushed outside. While he was gone, Sybilla shifted her position so he would have to walk under the hayloft to hand the water to her. He was soon back, so flustered that he did not notice she had moved. When he was near enough to hand her the flask, Sybilla jumped to her feet, grabbed the pole and leapt backwards, yanking it hard. With a terrible groan, the hayloft collapsed on the bandit, knocking him to the floor and burying him under beams and hay. Only his head and shoulder and one arm were visible, protruding from the wreckage.

The sight of the arm upset Sybilla. *What have I done?* she thought. *What if I've killed him?* Was it a mortal sin to kill a man in self-defence? True, the young man had kidnapped her, but he had not otherwise harmed her. Still, she was more concerned with saving her mortal life than her immortal soul at the moment.

She was about to flee the barn when she noticed that the thief wore a signet ring on his hand, with a family crest engraved on it. It took all her courage to kneel down and pull the ring off his finger — but she knew it might help identify her kidnappers later. She half expected him to grab her hand, but he did not stir. Breathing hard, she stood up, stuffed the ring in her pocket, then ran to the barn door and peeped out. There was a farmhouse nearby! Would the owners help her, or were they allies of her kidnappers? Something was wrong, though; there was no sign of life, no animals in the yard, and no smoke belching from the farmhouse chimneys. The whole place had a forlorn air. Had its inhabitants died of hunger because of the terrible drought, or had they abandoned the farm to seek work in a town?

When Sybilla saw that the coast was clear, she emerged cautiously. She had to get as far away from here as she could before the second thief returned. But which way was home? Trying to remember what Clement had taught her about finding her way, she squatted down in the dust of the farmyard and quickly scratched a map in the dirt. It was rather odd looking, but then she was never very good at drawing. She drew in Rouen, and Saint-Valery on the coast of Normandy. She sketched in the route between them, which she knew well from her visits home, and marked the crossroads. Then she drew a line north. If she'd been right about where they had ridden after they turned off at the crossroads, she would need to travel north-west — to her left — to get home.

Sybilla was about to stand up when a wet nose pressed against her face. "Hannibal!" She felt weak with gratitude. "Good dog. I knew you'd follow me." The hound barked happily. The sight of her bloodhound gave Sybilla an idea. Hannibal was an excellent tracker; he had found her in this godforsaken place, after all. Why not send him home to fetch her mother?

"Would you like to go and get Emma for me, Hannibal?" she asked. The dog gave a little whine and a short bark, so she went on. "I want you to find Emma and take this to her." She took Geoffrey's ring from the ribbon around her neck and put it on her finger. Then she looped the thief's ring onto the ribbon and tied it securely around Hannibal's neck. The dog barked. Next Sybilla took off her mother's pouch with the holy pebble in it and put it under the hound's nose. "EMMA!" she said. "Hannibal, find Emma!"

Hannibal whined and licked Sybilla's face. This wasn't working. She stood, and pointed in what she hoped was the direction of home. "Go! Find Emma!" she said sternly. The dog walked away, then came back and looked pleadingly at her. He didn't want to leave her alone in a strange place. Sybilla hated the thought herself, but she knew that if she weakened, Hannibal would never go. She hardened her voice and shouted angrily: "Go home now! Get Emma!"

Finally the years of obedience training took over, and Hannibal walked away. He looked back, but when Sybilla kept pointing, he bowed his head obediently then started to run. And she should do the same. Picking herself up, Sybilla brushed the straw and dust from her clothes and looked around for Merlin. Ah, there he was, up in a tree keeping watch. Suddenly she heard a faint groan from the barn. Her captor was alive! Relief flooded through her — as desperately as she wanted freedom, she did not wish to save her own life by taking another's. But this also meant she didn't have a moment to lose!

CHAPTER SIX

Sybilla walked briskly to take advantage of the waning light. It would be dark in a couple of hours, but she did not want to think about that. Perhaps she would find another deserted shack or farmhouse, or at worst a hedge or haystack to sleep in. It was a pity that Dancer had run off with her warm cloak. The thought of the cloak made her look at her clothing. Her veil was askew, showing her hair, and her mantle was streaked with dust. *What would Aunt Maud say if she could see this vagabond?* she wondered. *Would she even recognise me?*

But her appearance was the least of her worries. On she plodded across fields covered in weeds and brown grass, crossing the occasional track used by the field workers. When she came upon a copse of beech trees that was too big to walk around, she hesitated, remembering what had happened to her in the woods earlier. But as there was no choice, she plucked up her courage, picked up her skirts and set off into the trees at a run. Once she thought she heard a noise and took fright, but it turned out to be a hare, as fearful as she was.

On the other side of the copse, she found a shallow stream, and with a sigh of relief, threw herself down beside it. After having a long drink of muddy water, she soaked her sore feet. Though less than a day had passed, it seemed like weeks since she'd last had a decent meal, and she found herself daydreaming about roast beef, salty bacon, plump capon… Her mouth watered. Even a crisp apple and a piece of cheese would feel like a feast now.

Reluctantly, she banished thoughts of food and comfort from her mind, put her shoes back on, and continued on her way, praying that she was heading in the right direction. From time to time she saw peasants in the distance working on dusty plots of land, but she saw no horses or donkeys, and nobody with a cart on which she might beg a ride.

By the time darkness fell, Sybilla was exhausted, but fear kept her moving. She was growing desperate now for somewhere safe to spend the night. The moon rose, bathing the countryside in silver light. It was rather eerie, but Sybilla was comforted by the smiling face in the moon. It seemed to be showing her the way. Nonetheless, she picked her way carefully; she could not afford to fall and hurt herself.

Just as she was about to give up and lie down under a tree to sleep, she stumbled upon the ruins of a hut. A simple structure of rough planks, it was listing badly, and most of the roof had caved in. But it was better than the open air. Would it be empty, or would someone be sleeping in it? And would they be friendly? Sybilla edged closer, holding her breath, and peered in through the gaping hole where a door had been. Then she let out a breath: it was empty, save for a strong smell of sheep and dog. It must be an abandoned shepherd's hut.

Sybilla moved bits of wood aside and cleared a space for herself on the dirt floor, but it looked so cold and uninviting that she found a firm piece of wall and propped herself against it. If only Hannibal were here to keep her warm. With no one to see, she removed her veil and draped it over herself like a blanket. The discomfort, the moonlight through the roof and the stink of animals should have kept her awake, but she was asleep in minutes.

The next morning she was wakened by the sun shining in her eyes. She stared around, wondering where on earth she was. Then she remembered. In the harsh light of day the hut was even more squalid than she had thought, and seemed to be held up only by good luck and the weeds that had grown over the walls. But something was wrong. What was that horrible itch? Sybilla scrambled to her feet and examined her arms and legs. She was covered in ugly red lumps. Flea bites!

Without realising she had moved, she found herself outside the hut, slapping wildly at her clothes, trying to dislodge the fleas. When she calmed down, she sat on the ground and went carefully through her clothes, picking out the more tenacious vermin. Ugh! Fleas and lice and bugs made Sybilla's flesh crawl. When she seemed finally to be rid of them, she set off again.

Hungry and sore, she continued her weary trudge until, after an hour or so in which her fleabites warmed up and tortured her almost beyond endurance, a castle came into view. She paused to consider her options. Part of her longed to go there and throw herself on the mercy of the owner — anything to have a rest, a wash and a meal — but caution prevailed. She had no idea who owned the castle and where their loyalties lay. If they were allies of the English or even enemies of her father, she might simply be exchanging one peril for another. No, she was safer approaching a peasant or a town dweller. They would have no reason to harm her.

Skirting around the edge of a large wood, she slipped past the castle undetected. But before she was out of danger, a party of men on horseback rode out across its moat. She observed them anxiously. Which way would they go? Her way, it seemed. Her heart began to beat wildly, and she looked around for cover before they sighted her. Darting into the forest, she hid behind the trunk of a huge tree. *Stop panicking*, she told herself. *They can't possibly know you're here.*

But a worm of doubt wriggled in her brain. What if it was the kidnappers or their allies, out combing the countryside for her? On the riders came. They were getting frighteningly close when their leader held up his hand, signalling a halt. The horses whinnied and stamped as they were pulled up sharply. Up close she could see that the men were a scruffy, disreputable-looking bunch. Then their leader said something and pointed to the sky. They all looked up. Sybilla followed their gaze. Merlin! Her stomach plummeted. If they were looking for a falcon, they must be looking for her!

Please God, keep Merlin up in the heavens near you, she prayed. *Don't let him lead the hunters straight to me.* Then she had another thought: what if Emma had sent them? Maybe they were looking for her in order to rescue her? Perhaps she should approach them… She took one cautious step forward, about to reveal herself — then hesitated. None of them was from Saint-Valery, and they looked more like mercenaries than vassals. And if they were for hire, who would employ them but her kidnappers?

The men held a quick conference. Sybilla could only pick up fragments, but it was enough.

"… she even went in this direction?" asked one.

"Yeah, would she be able to find her way home?" said another.

"…no fool," said the leader, sounding impatient. "If she's smart enough to get away from Godfrey, she should be able to figure out how to get home."

Sybilla's heart jumped. Godfrey must be the young man who'd been guarding her. They were looking for her!

What if they decided to search the woods? Barely daring to breathe, Sybilla tried to make herself as small and still as possible behind the tree. But then God answered her prayers. One of the men cried out and pointed. It was Merlin — and instead of leading her pursuers straight to his mistress, he was hovering above a stand of trees some distance off! The leader gave a signal, and the men galloped off in pursuit of the bird.

It was not until the search party was just a small puff of dust in the distance that Sybilla found the courage to venture out into open country again. But she could not shake the dread of being pursued. When she had gone hunting herself, she had never stopped to wonder how her prey might feel. She had been consumed by the thrill of the chase and the sheer joy of pounding across the fields on a good horse on a fine morning. Now she knew what it felt like to be chased by men on horses. She wondered if she would ever be able to hunt again.

The thought brought her animals to mind. *What's happening to Dancer?* she fretted. *Will she find her way home to Saint-Valery when she has calmed down? Or has someone already captured her? And where is Hannibal? Did he understand what I wanted him to do? Did he set off for Saint-Valery?* And if he did, would he reach home safely before the kidnappers arrived to demand a ransom? And would he be able to lead Emma to her?

She tried to stop worrying, but when she thrust aside the visions of Dancer at a horse fair and Hannibal tied up in a barn somewhere, her mother's face took their place. She would be beside herself with worry by now. And what if she set out to look for Sybilla and ran into the English?

Her stomach rumbling with hunger and her head full of fears, Sybilla plodded on glumly, keeping a close watch on the path of the sun to make sure she was still heading west towards Saint-Valery. The land was more intensely cultivated here, a patchwork of small fields protected by windbreaks of beech trees. Staying out of sight was like trying to navigate through a maze. Not knowing what she would find in the next field was particularly nerve-racking. But if there were cultivated fields, there had to be people, she reasoned, and she might find someone willing to help her.

Eventually Sybilla saw smoke in the distance — a house! Hot and tired as she was, she quickened her pace. Perhaps the householder would have a spare donkey... although the way she felt now, a draught of water would do.

Then she heard an ominous baying sound in the distance. Dogs! She told herself it was a hunt — but it wasn't the hunting season. The sound grew louder. Sybilla recoiled in terror and looked around for help. Not a human being in sight. But there was a big old oak tree a field away. Fear gave her wings, and she flew to the tree. After hiking up her skirts and tying them in a knot between her legs, she shinnied up the tree and climbed as high as she could.

From her bird's-eye view in the oak, Sybilla watched in horror as a pack of wild dogs bore down on her hiding place. Half-starved, mangy and maddened by the scent of prey, they surrounded the tree. Some stood on their hind legs baying, trying desperately to reach her. Closing her eyes, she clung on, trembling, but she could still hear their claws raking the bark. She had never been so frightened in all her life. She had come off horses and fallen out of trees, but this was something she could never have imagined. It was like a nightmare.

Suddenly the dogs' barking changed. Sybilla opened her eyes to see a man walking across the field, accompanied by a big red dog. He was carrying a stout wooden staff. When he drew closer, Sybilla shouted for help. This enraged the dogs below, and their din made the man stop. His own dog began to run ahead, but the man whistled him back. Then he put his hand to his eyes to shade them, and stared up into the tree. Sybilla shouted again, as loudly as she could. This time the man heard her, and he charged at the dogs, flailing about him with his staff. His dog rushed at the pack, barking ferociously.

Threatened, some of the wild dogs turned and snarled at the man and his dog, ready to fight, while others stayed by the tree, growling at Sybilla to make sure their prey did not escape. But when the man bore down on them with his staff, the dogs suddenly formed themselves into a pack and fled, as if in answer to some secret signal. "You can come down now," he said, staring up at her. "They've gone."

"I know," said Sybilla, breathlessly. "But my legs won't work." In fact, they seemed to have turned to jelly.

"I can wait," said the man. He sat down in the shade of the tree, took a knife and a twig from his pocket, and began to whittle. Five minutes later Sybilla was sufficiently composed to climb down from the tree. As she dropped the last metre, the man got to his feet and smiled at her. The dog, which looked as if it had some wolf in it, growled.

"Down, Keeper," said the man. "She's a friend." The dog relaxed a little but remained watchful. Up close Sybilla's rescuer did not look like a hero. He was thin and sickly-looking, with knobbly wrists and eyes too big for his face. His grey hair was sparse, and most of his teeth were missing. "I'm Ralph," he said. "Who are you?"

"Sybilla de Saint-Valery, Monsieur," said Sybilla, surreptitiously scratching a bite on her arm. "Thank you for saving me."

"It was the Christian thing to do," the peasant replied. "But why is a lady like you out here in this field alone?"

"I'm trying to find my way home. I was kidnapped outside of Rouen, but I got away."

"Rouen is a long way, milady. You must be tired. Why don't you come to my house and rest?" He pointed at a small clump of cottages, with smoke coming from one of the chimneys. "It's over there."

Sybilla made no protest. What she really wanted to do was lie down in the field and sleep for the rest of her life. But there might be a horse or a donkey in Ralph's village. "Monsieur, I would like to buy a horse," she said.

"It's been a long time since we had a horse around here," he replied gloomily. Sybilla knew why when they reached the village. It was just a collection of dilapidated thatched huts, and looked almost deserted. The only living things seemed to be a few scrawny hens pecking dispiritedly in the dirt. In a normal village, everybody would have come out to inspect the stranger, and there would be goats and pigs and geese around. "What about a donkey?" Sybilla asked hopefully.

Ralph scratched his chin and pondered. "Robert the Redhead had a donkey, but he had to sell it. Then he used the money to leave here."

"Did everyone in the village go?" asked Sybilla.

"Just about. The ones that didn't starve first or die of the sickness, that is."

Sybilla had already witnessed the ravages of the drought, but what sickness was this man talking about?

"They call it Saint Anthony's Fire," he told her. "Purging and vomiting, awful pains in the head." He shook his head in wonder: "And it makes some folk think they can fly like angels."

Sybilla was shocked. She had heard of no sickness like this in the castle. "How many died, Monsieur?"

"Took ten of us, it did. Come along. I've got water and some bread. You're welcome to share it."

He led Sybilla into a dark, dirty hut. When her

eyes adjusted to the dimness, she saw that there was an ancient woman sitting on a three-legged milking stool by the fire.

"That's Mum," said Ralph. "Mum!" he shouted. "We've got ourselves a visitor."

The old lady woke from her doze, saw Sybilla and smiled beatifically. *So this was why Ralph had stayed home when others had left,* Sybilla thought. *He did not want to leave his poor old mother.* "You're a good man, Monsieur," she said. The words popped out of her mouth before she had time to think.

But instead of thinking her rude, he simply replied, "Jesus asked us to do unto others as we would have them do to us. That's what I try to do."

If I ever get home, I'll make sure these two are looked after, Sybilla vowed. *If I let them starve, I shall certainly go to Hell.* Mindful of the poverty of her hosts, Sybilla declined the offer of a crust of dry, hard-looking rye bread, despite her ravenous hunger. But the water was welcome, and she gulped it greedily.

Slightly revived, she took her leave of Ralph and his mother. "Am I going in the right direction to get to Saint-Valery?" she asked him.

He shrugged. "How would I know? I've never been more than a few leagues from here in my life."

"It's on the coast," Sybilla explained.

"In that case, I think you are."

Sybilla thanked Ralph and struck out for the west, following the sun. Keeper decided to go some of the way with her, and trotted along obediently at her side until he saw some quail. Unable to resist, he flushed them out of cover, then got the fright of his life as a falcon swooped out of the sky, plucked the quail from under his nose and wheeled off again. Sybilla looked around anxiously to see if Merlin had brought the hunting party with him, but there was no sign of mounted men. She heaved a sigh of relief.

Soon after, Keeper decided he'd strayed far enough from home and turned back. Sybilla was sorry to see him go. But she could not afford the luxury of self-pity with armed men out hunting for her. She quickened her pace.

Chapter Seven

The afternoon was wearing on. As she walked, Sybilla prayed to God to send her a donkey, or at least a highway. In some of the fields she passed, she saw peasants scavenging for food, but there was not an animal in sight. Her bites itched, her feet protested with every step, and her stomach felt as if it would cave in. Eventually she came upon an apple orchard, row after row of venerable old trees marching into the distance. At last, some shade! She threw herself down under a tree, startling a couple of crows, who complained raucously and flew off to a safe distance, from where they eyed her suspiciously.

After she had rested, she searched the orchard for an apple. Hungry people must have been here before her, though; all she found were a couple of grub-infested, wizened specimens. Who knew how long they had been lying there in the sun... But it was true, thought Sybilla — beggars can't be choosers.

She dug out the grubs with a stick and ate the fruit, which tasted sweet and slightly rotten, like cider.

Perhaps they were magic apples, or perhaps she was very tired, for she quickly fell into a doze and had vivid dreams. She dreamed that Geoffrey was there, offering her the little ring with the red stone. But when she reached out for it, he changed his mind. "No, Sybilla," he said sorrowfully. "You'll just swap it for a donkey."

Then her mother appeared, riding her favourite mare and dressed in travelling clothes. "Sybilla, where have you been?" she scolded. "I've searched the countryside for you, and here you are sleeping under an apple tree." Sybilla awoke with a start, expecting to see her mother bending over her, but she was alone. Her head ached, and she had a raging thirst. She struggled woozily to her feet, and tried to straighten her clothes. She was so hungry that she felt light-headed.

Then she heard a jangling noise and looked up. "Merlin!" she cried. "Where have you been?" The falcon alighted on the branch of an apple tree with a grasshopper in his beak. He politely offered it to Sybilla, who wished she had the stomach for insects. With Merlin perched on her wrist, she set out again.

Not long after, she realised that the dust under her feet had turned to grass. There must be water around! She started to run, startling her bird into flight, then tripped on the uneven ground and tumbled headlong down an incline into a slimy, stagnant pool. This must have been a stream once, but the drought had reduced it to a string of puddles.

Sybilla picked herself up and eyed the pond warily. Before today she would not have dreamed of drinking such polluted water, but she was desperate. After offering up a little prayer for courage, she scooped up a handful of the water and drank it. It tasted as foul as she had feared, but she managed to keep it and the next draught down. But when she took a third mouthful, something soft and disgusting wriggled in her mouth. She spat, and a small grey object flew through the air. It was a tadpole! She stepped back, shuddering. Merlin immediately swooped on the tadpole and ate it, and then took a bath in the scummy water, spraying her liberally with slime.

Now that she was wet, Sybilla decided to make the most of it. She took off her shoes to inspect her sore feet. As she had feared, they were red, swollen and blistered. Shooing Merlin out of the way, she waded into the pond and let the cool mud squelch up between her toes. It felt wonderful. Reluctantly she dried her feet on the grass and put her shoes back on. It was sheer torture, but the ground was too rough to walk barefooted.

Just then, Sybilla felt a reverberation under her feet. Horses were coming! Merlin heard them too and flew off into a tree. Sybilla looked around frantically, but there was nowhere to hide, and her feet hurt too much to run. She was trapped!

In moments they were upon her. There were four of them, but they were not from the hunting party she had run into earlier; they were soldiers, dressed for battle. With their unfamiliar clothing and their foreign looks, they must be English, she thought. Her blood curdled. All her life she had been hearing horror stories about the English, and now they were here and she was at their mercy!

Another quick look showed her that they had been out foraging for food. One had trussed chickens dangling from his pommel; the other had a squealing pig over his saddle. She wondered how they had found anything to steal in this blighted countryside. All these thoughts went through her head in a split second as she scrambled to her feet and tried to straighten her clothing and veil.

The leader of the English scouting party was a tall man with a long nose and piercing blue eyes, which surveyed her keenly. This lieutenant and one of his men held a murmured conversation, after which he asked Sybilla a question. Sybilla recognised some of the words, but his accent was thick, and there were other words she had never heard before. But it was likely that he wanted to know who she was and what she was doing here. Sybilla almost blurted out her name, but then some sixth sense told her to keep quiet. If she admitted to being a Saint-Valery, the English might well deduce she was related to Bernard de Saint-Valery, the Duke's most illustrious knight. If they did, they could decide to take her hostage and use her against her father and the Duke.

Sybilla decided to play dumb. If they thought she was just an ignorant country girl, they might decide she was not worth the trouble. The lieutenant looked her up and down, and narrowed his eyes. What was he thinking? Then she understood. Even though she looked a fright, a discerning eye could tell that her clothes were cut from fine cloth, not the coarse material of a peasant's tunic, and beneath all the grime her shoes were made of fine leather. This shrewd officer clearly suspected that she was no farm girl, even if she was dirty and unkempt.

He gave her some sort of order, then realised he was wasting his breath. Reaching down, he gestured with his head, letting her know he wanted her to climb up behind him. Sybilla's heart missed a beat. Where was he taking her? Would she end up in the hands of a Norman lord who owed loyalty to the King of England? But with armed soldiers surrounding her, it would be useless to resist. She grabbed his hand, put her foot in the stirrup and swung onto the horse behind the lieutenant. She could not believe she was being abducted a second time; if she lived to tell this tale, nobody would believe it. The Normans who had taken her prisoner yesterday — how long ago it seemed now! — had frightened her, but they had not been cruel, she realised now. The skinny pockmarked thief was rough and nasty, but the young gentleman had gone out of his way to make sure she was comfortable — and she had repaid him by bringing a hayloft down on his head… She doubted the English army would be so easy to trick.

The country they rode through was eerily empty. It was as if an ill wind had risen and blown its inhabitants away. Eventually they came to a lightly wooded hill and rode up it. At the top, cunningly hidden in a stand of trees, was a tent in a clearing. This must be an English encampment. But except for Sybilla's party and a few guards, it too was empty. *Everybody else must be out fighting the Duke's army,* she thought.

When they halted and dismounted, Sybilla could see why the English had made camp here. The hill overlooked a vast expanse of countryside, which meant they would be able to see strangers coming for leagues. Sybilla's captor dismounted, handed her down politely from the horse, and gestured for her to sit. *What now?* she wondered. She soon found out, for the lieutenant went into one of the tents and returned with some leather thongs, which he tied securely around her wrists and ankles. A flush of humiliation rose from Sybilla's toes to the tip of her head. She felt like a turkey trussed for the oven! Worse, she had no idea where she was. If by chance Hannibal reached home and fetched Emma, would they ever be able to track her to this place? And if they did, would her mother dare try to rescue her from the English army?

After watering their horses and tying the pig to a

tree, Sybilla's captors set about making themselves a meal. They lit a fire, roasted two of the chickens and gobbled them down with gusto. The aroma made Sybilla feel faint with longing — and angry. But then the reality of her situation hit her. She was a prisoner of war. As an enemy, she had no right to food or sympathy. And she doubted that Norman soldiers would act any differently towards their captives.

Sybilla had thought fear would keep her alert, but her body was weary from the hours of walking. Sleep eventually overtook her and she toppled onto her side. Some time later a hubbub awoke her, and she struggled upright, stiff and sore from her awkward position. Then she saw why the guards were agitated: there was a cloud of dust on the horizon. It turned into a company of riders heading towards the encampment. Her heart began to beat faster. The English soldiers readied themselves for the worst, but as the riders neared the camp, a keen-sighted guard shouted something, and everyone relaxed.

Everyone but Sybilla, that is, for it meant that more English soldiers were approaching. She had the impression that her captors were waiting for someone who had the authority to decide her fate. If this man hated all Normans indiscriminately, he might execute her as a spy; if he was the sort of man to take pity on a lost girl, he might let her go. But how could she persuade him that she was harmless when they could not speak each other's language?

When the English company rode up, Sybilla saw that they were led by a knight, a huge man with red hair like a Viking. She tensed, expecting him to approach her. But he clearly had more important things on his mind, and from the way he gestured to the other soldiers, it seemed he was calling a conference in his tent.

By the time the knight got around to inspecting the captive, the sun had risen much higher in the sky. Sybilla had found the tension almost unbearable, but the sight of the redhead and his retinue striding towards her was even worse than the wait. Towering over her, he crossed his arms over his barrel chest and stared down with ice-cold green eyes. Then he signalled to one of the soldiers, who quickly pulled Sybilla to her feet and undid the bindings on her ankles.

In a harsh voice used to giving orders, the knight asked her a question. Sybilla hung her head. He said something and his men laughed. Then the redhead came closer and walked around her. First he felt the fabric in her tunic, then took hold of her hands in his huge paws and examined them. His soldiers stood in a circle, intrigued. What was he doing? Then Sybilla understood: her hands would tell him if she was a lady or a peasant. Although they were dirty and her nails broken, they were soft. She had never had to grub in the soil to grow food, or chop wood for the fire. And of course, she was still wearing Geoffrey's ring. Satisfied, the knight dropped her hands, looked into her eyes and smiled knowingly. Then he barked an order to the soldier who had captured her, turned on his heel and strode off.

The drama over, the soldiers dispersed. What had he said? What would happen to her now? Sybilla felt weak with trepidation. But she did not have to wait long to discover her fate. The lieutenant unbound her hands, which tingled painfully as the blood rushed back, and led her to his horse. He mounted, pulled her up behind him, and they set off down the hill. Where were they headed? Sybilla tried to get her bearings, and it seemed to her that they were going in the direction from which the knight and his company had come.

Perhaps they were on their way to the English headquarters. If they were, it meant that they did have plans for her. The thought that they might use her to bring her father to his knees made her feel ill, and the rocking motion of the horse did not help. The jangle of the horse's bridle reminded her that she had not seen Merlin for hours. She looked up anxiously, and was comforted to see him, high up in the heavens, keeping her company.

The lieutenant broke in on her thoughts, saying something and pointing. They were approaching an imposing stone castle, its perimeter heavily guarded by English soldiers. They must have taken this castle from a Norman lord! If the English army had the force to take such a substantial castle, they must be strong, Sybilla thought, with a thrill of fear. What would be next — Saint-Valery? Or even the Duke's castle at Rouen?

Inside the walls, it was obvious that the castle had been turned into an English base. There were soldiers everywhere, and the only remaining Normans were servants, who scuttled about doing their new masters' bidding with frightened eyes. Where was the lord of this domain? Away fighting with the Duke, or imprisoned in his own dungeon? Sybilla shivered. Was that where she would end up too?

It seemed so. After conferring with a senior officer, the lieutenant handed Sybilla over to a guard, who marched her through the castle forecourt and down some stone steps into a long dark room with thick, dank stone walls and a flagstone floor. There she was passed into the care of a turnkey, who pushed her into a small, dimly lit room. The heavy door slammed shut with a horribly final thud, and a key turned in the lock.

It took her eyes a few minutes to adjust to the gloom, but when they did, Sybilla saw that she was in a small cell that contained only a wooden bench. A narrow slit high in the wall let in some greyish light. She could hear water dripping somewhere. Although the sun had been shining outside, it was freezing in the cell, and she could feel the cold coming up through her thin shoes. She had never liked small, confined spaces, and this one was dark, damp and cold as well. It was like being buried alive. *What if they forget I'm here?* she agonised.

For the first time since she had left Rouen, Sybilla felt too desolate even to pray. In this bleak moment of the soul, she lost all track of time. It might have been minutes or hours later that the sound of a key in the door roused her from her despair. Then the door crashed back, and she was being manhandled out of the cell and up the steps by a guard.

Blinded by the daylight, she had no idea where she was going, and stumbled. The guard shouted something at her, pulled her upright and dragged her into the castle. They passed through the Great Hall, which was not as grand as the Duke's but more ornate than the one at home, and stopped in front of a massive door. The guard handed her over to a sentry and left. The sentry knocked on the door. It opened, and a soldier took hold of Sybilla and pulled her inside.

She was in the castle armoury. Sunlight from the high windows glinted off the coats of armour and weaponry that lined the walls, hurting her eyes. Then she saw that she was standing in front of a man seated in an ornately carved throne-like chair. The first thing she noticed about him was his extraordinary beauty. He had longish fair hair, a straight nose and eyes so dark they were almost black. When he stood up, she saw that he was not particularly big or tall, but he was fit and well-muscled. His clothing, which was clearly expensive, fitted him like a glove.

The man stared at her for a long moment, a strange expression on his face. Then he said: "Mademoiselle, please sit down." His Languedor was perfect, with no trace of an accent.

Surprised, Sybilla sat down in the chair he'd indicated.

"I know you understand me, so don't pretend you don't," he said. "My men have brought you here because they think you are a lady. Are you?"

Sybilla remained as mute as stone. She would not cooperate with the English against her own countrymen. Her determination must have shown on her face, because the knight laughed. It was such an odd reaction that Sybilla — who had been expecting an angry response — sat up and stared at him.

"Let me tell you a story," he began, seemingly oblivious to her dumbfounded expression. "There was once a young Norman lord training to be a knight in the castle of one of Normandy's grandest lords. While he was still a squire, a girl came to live at the castle. She was pretty, yes, but that was not what made her so attractive to him. It was her spirit and determination. She was better at most games than the pages and squires at the castle, and she rode better than most men."

Sybilla, who had been wondering where all this was going, pricked up her ears. He could have been describing her. But the knight was still talking. "The Norman lord had been promised to the daughter of an immensely rich and powerful nobleman when he was just an infant, but he fell in love with the girl at the castle. Because he suspected she returned his feelings, he told her one day that he loved her." The knight's voice trailed away, and he seemed lost in his memories for a moment. "It was a cruel thing to do, as she was about to be married."

He broke off suddenly, then returned to the present. "And you're sitting there wondering what all this has got to do with you."

Sybilla gave a little start. Could he read her mind?

"Would it give you a clue if I told you the girl's name was Emma, and that she went on to marry Bernard de Saint-Valery?" he asked.

The shock was so great that Sybilla leapt to her feet. A sentry started forward, but the knight waved him back. "And you're her daughter, no?" he asked.

Speechless, Sybilla nodded. "I suspected it the moment you walked in here," he said. "You have her eyes, and you move the way she did. But it was that mulish look on your face that convinced me. I've seen that expression on Emma's face many times. You're taller, though."

"That comes from my father," said Sybilla,

unable to resist a minute longer. Her voice felt rusty from disuse.

When she spoke, the knight smiled. "What on earth were you doing out in the countryside by yourself?"

The smile told Sybilla this man was her friend. The floodgates opened, and she poured out her story. The knight sat in silence, shaking his head as he listened. "I'm sure your mother must be scouring the countryside for you," he said when she had finished. "Riding one of those fine Arab steeds of hers."

Sybilla's eyebrows flew up.

"I have one of them," he explained. "I own land on both sides of the Channel, so I move back and forth between England and Normandy." He paused. "It pains me that your family and I are on opposite sides."

Sybilla did not want to talk about the war. "So my mother has seen you again?" she asked.

He nodded. "It was wrong of me, but I couldn't stop myself."

"Did she… Did she…" Sybilla began, but could not continue.

The knight smiled. "You want to know if she returned my affections? I'm afraid you'll have to ask her that yourself."

Did that mean…?

"I'm letting you go," he said, answering her unspoken question.

Sybilla gaped at him.

"My men will take you to a road that leads to Saint-Valery. But from there you're on your own. I have a war to fight."

Sybilla finally came to her senses. "Thank you, milord."

The knight rose and accompanied her to the door. Sybilla knew she was taking a risk, but she couldn't leave without knowing who this extraordinary man was. "When my mother finds me, who shall I say let me go?" she asked.

He grinned. "You're your mother's daughter, all right. Tell her that Guy de Saint-Pol sends his regards."

Chapter Eight

Within an hour Sybilla found herself unceremoniously dumped on the side of a road by an English soldier. "Which way is Saint-Valery?" she asked.

Not able to understand her, or not caring, the man shrugged and galloped off. For a moment Sybilla felt deflated, but then her spirits rose. A road meant travellers, and travellers meant horses and mules and donkeys. She stared left then right, wondering which direction to take. While she hesitated, a dark dot appeared on the horizon. As she watched, it grew bigger, and eventually revealed itself to be two people on a donkey cart.

As the cart drew closer, Sybilla saw that it had a second donkey tethered to the back. Emboldened, she stepped into the road. "Whoa!" said the driver, and the cart came to a halt. The man was large, with a ruddy face and grey whiskers, and the boy beside him, who looked about twelve, was too much like him to be anything but his son. The two of them stared mutely at this apparition. Sybilla could almost hear them thinking, *Not another beggar.* She was right, for the man shouted "Giddyap!", and the donkey began to move.

Desperate, Sybilla grabbed hold of the reins. "I'm not a beggar," she said. "I want to buy your donkey."

The boy laughed, but the man's contemptuous expression turned cunning. He had guessed from Sybilla's accent that she was well-born. "Who are you?" he demanded.

Sybilla had learned caution in the last two days and saw no reason to trust this man. He would probably betray her to the first person who offered him a reward. "It doesn't matter who I am," she said haughtily. "What matters is that I want a donkey and I can pay for it."

This was a different kettle of fish altogether. Scenting a profit, the man and the boy exchanged a calculating look. *They mean to cheat me,* thought Sybilla, outraged. "Well, are you going to sell me the donkey?" she asked.

"What will you give me for it?" asked the man, a rapacious gleam in his eye.

Sybilla put out her hand. "This ring."

"And what else?" demanded the man.

His greed made Sybilla's hackles rise. *He's just a common thief,* she thought. *This ring is worth a herd of donkeys. And a new cart!* "Nothing else," she said. "It's all I have."

Their eyes locked. The man clearly wanted the ring, and Sybilla needed the donkey. But there were two of them, and they were stronger. If they decided to take the ring by force, there would be little she could do. She knew she must not show fear. "I want some food, too," she said.

The boy looked at his father and, when he nodded, took a cloth bag from the cart and handed it to Sybilla. In it were a slab of bread, a flask of ale and an apple. "This is all we've got," said the boy. "We're on our way home."

"It will do," said Sybilla. Meanwhile, his father had jumped down from the cart and untethered the donkey from the back. When the donkey protested, he gave it a slap on the flank, and dragged it into the roadway. He passed the beast's reins to Sybilla with one hand and thrust out the other for the ring. The exchange was made. Sybilla's heart lurched as his dirty fist closed over her keepsake. Geoffrey had only been gone a few days and already she had betrayed him. Would he ever forgive her? Choking down her emotion, she asked: "Which way is Saint-Valery?"

The man pointed back in the direction he had come. "That way. When you get to the crossroads about two leagues down, turn left." Sybilla could not bring herself to thank him. She waited till the cart had gone, then took a long drink of ale, and gobbled down the bread and the apple. The food did wonders for her sense of wellbeing, and her spirits rose. She mounted the donkey, turned it around and set off slowly along the road. Though it was painfully slow, it was bliss to be off her tortured feet. *I've certainly come down in the world,* she thought ruefully. *From Dancer to this!* Then she remembered that Christ rode into Jerusalem on a donkey on Palm Sunday, and felt guilty for her sin of pride.

They plodded on, with Sybilla fighting off sleep. If she were very lucky, she might come upon a safe place before it got too dark. It was not a good idea to be on the road at night. Especially a road like this, dark and overhung on both sides by trees. It was like riding through a tunnel.

If only Hannibal was here, she thought. *He could run ahead and scout out danger and warn me.* But

Hannibal had more important work to do. He might even have reached Saint-Valery and be leading her mother to her by now. If he hadn't been brought down by wild dogs. Or stolen. Sybilla pushed these sombre visions aside; she had to trust that help was coming.

It was dark now. The donkey was restive, and Sybilla wondered what he could hear or smell out there in the shrouded countryside. Then, as the beast plodded up a rise, the moon appeared miraculously at the end of the tunnel of trees. It must have been an omen, for just as she was about to give up hope of finding shelter, Sybilla saw a derelict hut by the roadside. Holding the donkey tightly by the reins, she peered in through the doorway: the door had long gone. Evidently she was not the first person to find sanctuary here, for there was a heap of dirty straw in a corner, and a pile of chicken bones.

Sybilla longed to throw herself down on the straw and sleep. But what should she do with the donkey? If she tied it up outside, it might be stolen or attacked by dogs. Eventually she brought it into the hut and attached its reins to a post. As soon as her body hit the smelly straw, she fell into a deep, exhausted sleep. Then something woke her. At first she did not know where she was, but then she remembered. In a hut with a donkey. Or she had been, for the donkey was gone. It must have been the beast's departure that had woken her, she realised.

She jumped to her feet and rushed out of the hut, looking around frantically. Then she saw them: two figures running down the road dragging the donkey, lit by the moon. It was the peasant and his son, of course. They hadn't been content to cheat her on the price; now they had stolen the donkey back as well! Rage welled up in Sybilla. How dare they! She looked around for a weapon, but could not find anything, not even a tree branch.

I'll never get home now, she thought. It was too much. Throwing herself down on the straw, she gave in to despair, sobbing as if she would never stop. But what was that noise? She sat up and strained her ears: there was definitely something going on outside. Tears forgotten, she went to the door of the hut and looked out. But a cloud had drifted across the moon and turned the world dark and she could scarcely see the nose in front of her face.

Then the sound of galloping horses reached her through the night. And weren't those flaming torches? The horses' hooves stopped suddenly, and a donkey brayed in fear. A dog barked hysterically and men shouted. Somebody had bailed up the thieves! But who? Sybilla stepped cautiously out of the hut, curious but poised for flight. Just then the moon broke through the clouds and illuminated the scene in front of her. Somebody caught sight of her and shouted. Panic-stricken, Sybilla erupted from the hut and bolted into the fields. The dog chased her, barking, and a horse came galloping after the dog.

Then a familiar voice called, "Sybilla, stop! It's me! And Hannibal." It was her mother. A body threw itself at her, pushing her to the ground, and slobbered all over her face. Crying and laughing, she shouted: "Stop it, you silly dog!" Then she was pulled to her feet, and enfolded in her mother's arms.

"Thank God we've found you," said Emma de Saint-Valery, in a voice trembling with relief. She took off her cloak and put it around her shivering daughter. "Come, let's get you home."

Sybilla fell asleep against her mother's back on the grey mare and could never remember a thing about the journey home. Nor did she remember being put to bed, where she slept away another day. When she awoke, she found Hannibal asleep beside her, his head on her chest. Her movement woke him, and he immediately began to lick her face. Wide awake now, she roughed up his coat and pulled his ears, making him sigh.

Then the events of the last two days flooded into her mind. *Was it all just a horrible nightmare, or had it really happened?* she asked herself. When she got out of bed, the pain told her it had been real. Her feet were tender and blistered — and disgustingly dirty. The first order of business was a hot bath in front of the fire and a set of fresh clothing. How luxurious it felt to be clean! Her mother had hovered for a while, but when she saw that Sybilla had suffered no lasting damage, went off to attend to business. She returned in time to join her daughter at the table for the first decent meal she'd had in days.

While Sybilla ate ravenously, she told her mother all that had happened to her. She left out nothing, and praised the courage and kindness of Ralph, who had rescued her from the wild dogs. To her pleasure, Emma immediately decided to despatch a messenger to take him a reward. "Not money, Mama," Sybilla advised. "They need food. They're starving."

Finally Sybilla recounted being picked up by the English patrol. "They took me to a castle, and threw me in the dungeon. Then I was brought before the commandant." When she described the knight who had questioned her, her mother's eyes widened and her hands flew to her face. "And then he let me go, and had me taken to a roadway," Sybilla concluded.

"This knight, did he say why he was letting you go?" asked Emma.

Until now, Sybilla hadn't been sure just what she would say if her mother asked this question, but suddenly she knew. It was their secret, Emma and Guy's, not hers. And as the daughter of Bernard de Saint-Valery, not of Guy de Saint Pol, it was none of her business. *God will forgive one little white lie,* she thought. "No, Mama. But before I left he told me his name. It was Guy de Saint-Pol."

At the sound of the name, Emma smiled as if she'd already guessed. Her face softened, and Sybilla knew that Emma had returned Guy's feelings, that he had been to her what Clement was to Eleanor — her first love. But Sybilla knew that Emma had learned to love Bernard de Saint-Valery. Her parents' marriage was a good one. So perhaps she would learn to love Geoffrey, and Eleanor could be happy raising pigs and children with Alan Peverel — if she did not run away with Clement.

The thought of Geoffrey reminded Sybilla of a secret of her own — that she had bought the donkey with Geoffrey's ring. But she was still too ashamed of losing it to a thief to confess it to Emma.

When Sybilla hesitated, Emma began to tell her side of the story. She had ridden out to meet her daughter, but had grown alarmed when she had not turned up. She was on her way home when she caught sight of Hannibal running through a field and called him. "He was in a terrible state, exhausted and terribly thirsty. And when I found the signet ring I knew you'd sent him home with a message."

"Whose ring is it, Mama, do you know?"

Her mother nodded. "It's the insignia of the Montmorency family. It must have been Gilbert who had you kidnapped. He's the villain who tried to take the estate from me when your father was away years ago." She smiled grimly. "I beat him that time, and I've beaten him again."

"What happened next, Mama?"

"I went home to call our men together to go after you, but before we left, an ugly little man with pockmarks turned up demanding ransom."

"What did he want?"

"He said that his master — he had no idea that I knew it was Gilbert — would exchange you for the deeds to the estate."

Sybilla's jaw dropped — it was just as she had feared. "But they didn't have me to swap, Mama! I'd already escaped by then."

"But I didn't know that, and neither did he. And he didn't know I had Hannibal. I had a big decision to make. Should I hold the messenger, or give him the deeds? If I held the messenger, would Gilbert panic and…" She could not finish the sentence.

And get rid of the evidence, thought Sybilla, turning cold.

Her mother noticed, and put an arm around her daughter. "But I decided to trust Hannibal to find you. After all, I'd trained him myself, and I know he would die for you."

At first light, Emma had set out with her little army and the exhausted Hannibal on the saddle in front of her. "We had to move fast," she explained. "We had to find you before Gilbert realised that we had his accomplice locked in our dungeon."

When they reached the crossroads where Sybilla's abductors had turned off the main road, Hannibal began to bark. They put him down and let him run. "You should thank your hound, Sybilla," her mother said. "Tired as he was, he led us all the way back to the barn where he'd left you."

When they found the barn deserted, Emma gave Hannibal one of Sybilla's old cloth dolls to sniff and told him to track her down. Hannibal found the scent quickly and after that it was just a matter of time. The bloodhound became very agitated when he found the oak where the wild dogs had treed his mistress, and had to be quietened. Then he led them to Ralph's hut.

"Your friend Ralph didn't tell us he'd rescued you, but he did tell us which way you'd gone, and we followed you to a pond. After that Hannibal lost the scent."

"Because I was on the Englishman's horse," said Sybilla. "How did you find me again?"

"I took a chance and headed for the road to Saint-Valery. I just had to trust that nothing terrible had happened to you, and that you'd find your way there, too. As we hadn't found you before we left the road, I decided to search further south this time. I was about to give up when I heard Merlin's bells. He must have recognised us and come down to look. Then he flew off again, so we followed him. When he landed on the roof of the hut, we guessed you were in there."

Sybilla felt a twinge of guilt. She'd been so exhausted that she had completely forgotten about

Merlin. Her mother must have guessed, for she said: "He followed us home, by the way."

"Thank you, Mama."

Her mother nodded. "And then those two men came running out of the hut, so we chased them. We thought they were the kidnappers, but they were just ordinary thieves. But we didn't know who might be in the hut with you…"

"And then I ran out into the field," said Sybilla.

"And when my men looked in the hut, there was no one there. So we knew it was all over."

"But it's not, is it, Mama? What will happen to the men who kidnapped me?"

"We've got one of them, and it won't be hard to find the injured one. Word will quickly reach Gilbert de Montmorency that you're home safe and that I have one of his men. If he's got any sense, he'll leave the duchy, because when Bernard comes back, his life won't be worth living."

Catching the look on Sybilla's face, Emma said: "Your father *will* be back, Sybilla." She put her hand over her daughter's. "And so will Geoffrey."

At that, Sybilla lowered her head in shame. "Oh, Mama, I exchanged Geoffrey's ring for that donkey. I wonder if he'll ever forgive me."

"I wouldn't worry about that if I were you," said her mother. "I know he'd prefer you safe and well to a ring, any day. And when he returns, it will be an excuse to give you another."

Relieved, Sybilla threw herself into her mother's arms. Feeling left out, Hannibal hurled himself between them, barking. The two women laughed. "Time to get to work," said Emma. "There is someone waiting for you in the stables. She turned up yesterday…"

"Dancer!" cried Sybilla.

Sybilla was glad to be home, but at the back of her mind, as she helped her mother around the house and in the stables, was the constant worry about her father and Geoffrey. The helplessness was the worst. The men had to fight, but all she and Emma could do was pray.

———❧———

It was nearly a month later that Sybilla, out exercising the horses with one of the grooms, heard the pounding of hooves in the distance. She stiffened, frightening the horse, which neighed and reared. *The English!* she thought, fighting to bring the horse under control. The prospect of being captured again filled her with panic. Then a party of horsemen appeared at the top of a rise, and someone shouted something. She wheeled the horse around to flee, but the groom put his hand out and grabbed the reins, stopping her. He was grinning. *Why is the fool grinning?* Sybilla wondered. Then the voice sounded again, and she realised that it was calling her name. She looked up to see a horseman cut away from the pack and race towards her, whooping. He was big and blond, with a red beard.

"Papa!" Sybilla shouted and galloped towards him.

Bernard de Saint-Valery brought good news and bad from the battlefield. Geoffrey had survived, and Bellême and Barneville had been spared, but the English had won the war. King William had trounced the Norman forces and annexed some of the Duke's lands, and was already moving his allies into the castles the English forces had captured.

God had been merciful to the Saint-Valerys this time. Sybilla had reached home safely; Bernard had lived to fight again; and the family had hung onto their lands. But as long as the Duke and his brother remained at loggerheads, the threat of war would hang over Normandy. In the meantime, life would go on. Sybilla would marry Geoffrey and move to

Bellême, and one day her own daughter would listen wide-eyed to her mother's amazing tale of abduction, adventure and rescue, and dream of the handsome knight who had loved her grandmother and set her mother free.

AUTHOR'S NOTE

France as we know it now did not exist in the eleventh century. Phillip I called himself the King, but in fact he controlled only a small area around Paris. The rest of the country was ruled by dukes and counts who were often more powerful than the King. France did not even have a common language then; in the north the people spoke Languedor, and in the south, Languedoc.

Normandy was one of the most powerful duchies in what we now know as France. The Normans — or northmen — were descended from the original tribes who lived in the north-west (Neustria), and the Vikings who launched a series of invasions from Scandinavia between the ninth and eleventh centuries. At the time this story takes place, the Normans ruled an empire. William the Conqueror had vanquished the English in 1066, and the Normans had also conquered the south of Italy.

In the story, Sybilla's father is called up by the Duke of Normandy to help repel an invasion by his brother, King William II of England. The enmity between the two brothers started when their father, William the Conqueror, bequeathed the throne of England to his middle son William instead of his oldest son, Robert. Robert was instead bequeathed Normandy, a lesser prize.

After the Norman conquest of England, there were Norman lords on both sides of the English Channel, some of them loyal to William, others to Robert. Under Robert, Normandy was in a state of anarchy, with barons defying his authority, waging private wars and building castles without permission. William, on the other hand, ruled England with a rod of iron.

Perhaps because they preferred Robert's easygoing ways, Norman knights from both countries revolted against William, but Robert failed to show up in England to rally his supporters, and the King was able to quell the rebellion. In 1090 William invaded Normandy, and it is this war that Sybilla's father and fiancé are going off to fight. William crushed his brother's forces, and forced him to hand over some of his land. When Robert needed money to go to the

First Crusade in the Holy Land in 1096, the two made peace, and the King lent the Duke 10 000 marks of silver in return for the right to Normandy and its revenues for five years.

When William II died in a hunting accident in 1100, Robert should have inherited the throne of England, but he was still on his way home from the crusade. His younger brother Henry seized the crown. Robert invaded England the following year, but Henry defeated him and forced him to renounce his claim to the throne of England. The peace did not last. Henry invaded Normandy in 1105 and, after decisively defeating Robert's army at the Battle of Tinchebray, claimed Normandy as a possession of the English crown. Robert was captured in battle and imprisoned for life. He died in 1134 in Cardiff Castle and was buried in what is now Gloucester Cathedral.

Life in a medieval castle

There were about 20 000 castles in France in the eleventh century. Their owners were kings of their own domains. They had their own banners, courts of law and subjects. When danger threatened, the lord would let down the drawbridge and allow his subjects to take refuge inside the castle walls. In return for his protection, the people had to do certain amounts of free labour on the estate. This system of rights and duties is called feudalism.

Nestled against the castle were outbuildings such as stables, kennels, the falconry, sheep pens and servants' quarters. The serfs, or tenant farmers, lived here. The estate was largely self-contained, producing bread made from home-grown corn and rye, butter and cheese from the dairy, bacon from its pigs, and even candles. Some of the linen and clothes worn by members of the household was spun and woven there.

A lord employed a number of officials to help him run his estate. His steward, the role filled by Roger de Barneville in this story, was the most important and powerful of these. He organised the work on the farm, kept the castle's accounts and presided over the court when the lord was away. The bailiff was next in importance. Although he was a peasant, he was a freeholder — that is, he owned his own farm. He allotted jobs to the peasants or serfs, looked after the cattle, and maintained the buildings. The reeve was the bailiff's assistant. He was a peasant, chosen by the other serfs; he supervised work and made sure nothing was stolen.

Most of the castles in Normandy in Sybilla's day would have consisted of a square wooden tower called a keep built on an earthen mound and surrounded by a moat and wooden palisades (fence). If a lord's enemies breached the palisades, they could starve out the inhabitants of the keep, or burn it down. The Duke of Normandy and his lords would have had stone castles. They were much easier to defend than the wooden variety: they could not be burned down, and had small narrow windows from which to fire arrows, and battlements from which the defenders could rain down fire or boiling oil on the enemy below.

On the ground floor of a medieval castle were the bakery, the kitchen, the Great Hall, the court room and the bailiff's room. The Great Hall was the hub. Here the lord held court, giving orders to his officials and sentencing wrongdoers to punishment. The pages did their lessons in the Great Hall, and everybody dined there. After the meal, the noble family retired to their chambers and everybody else slept on straw on the stone floor.

Nearby was the armoury, which was the finest room in the castle. It was decorated with weapons, ornate helmets, breastplates, etc., and it was here that the lord received homage from his vassals. This floor also contained the chapel, with the lord's ancestors buried in its walls. The first floor contained rooms for use by the warriors and the bedrooms of the lord's family. The bedrooms were furnished with a bed, a clothes chest which also served as a seat, and a prayer stool. The beds were huge, and often a lord would invite some of his knights to share his bed, along with his wife and his dogs.

The lady of the manor's bedroom boasted rich wall hangings, large wooden chests and upholstered armchairs; the rest were very plain. Floors were made of flagstones or tiles. In winter they were covered with straw; in summer they were sprinkled with aromatic herbs. Beneath the castle were the dungeons where criminals or the lord's enemies were imprisoned, with the soldiers' guard room above.

The education of children

In Sybilla's time the children of the aristocracy were sent off to the households of their parents' friends or political allies — the girls to learn etiquette and how to run a household, the boys to learn the duties of a lord of the manor.

In the Middle Ages, marriage was a business contract. Girls married at about fourteen. Fathers arranged marriages for their children, and they were betrothed at a young age, sometimes even in the cradle. Women who did not find a husband ended up in a convent.

A boy started off at about seven as a page, became a squire at fourteen, and could become a knight at twenty-one. Some boys started training to be soldiers at a young age, others combined soldiering with running their own estates. Men like Sybilla's father Bernard were vassals as well as knights. This meant they owed military service to their liege lord in return for his protection. A knight like Bernard would have been away fighting for the Duke for about six months each year.

Sybilla's animals

Many ladies of Sybilla's rank hunted with hawks or falcons. Falconry had its own rules and customs. For example, the gyrfalcon was for the king, the peregrine for an earl, the bastard hawk for a baron, the lanner and lanneret for a squire, the merlin for a lady, the tercel for a poor man, the sparrowhawk for a priest and the kestrel for a servant or a knave. Birds used in falconry are divided into long wings (falcons) which hunt birds and short wings (hawks) that hunt a range of prey, mostly rabbits. Sybilla's Merlin was a long wing. Falconry is still a sport in some countries such as the United Kingdom, but it is prohibited in Australia and New Zealand.

The bloodhound, or the Saint Hubert's Hound, was the most popular hunting dog in France in the Middle Ages. Though they are affectionate and gentle with children, these dogs are also energetic and boisterous, and can be wilful. Like Hannibal, they howl, snore and drool a lot. Bloodhounds can follow any scent, including that of humans, and can pick up a trail 100 hours old, and have been known to stay on a trail for 200 kilometres.

Normandy was famous for its thoroughbred horses, which had been bred from Arab and Berber steeds introduced into the Iberian Peninsula (now Spain and Portugal) by the Moors (North Africans) when they invaded in the eighth century. It is quite possible that Emma de Saint-Valery fitted in running a horse stud around her other duties.

If Sybilla had eaten the rye bread that Ralph offered her in his hut, she might have ended up with the sickness that had already killed ten people in the village. What in the Middle Ages was called Saint Anthony's Fire — or "holy fire" or "hell fire" — is now known as "ergotism", a disease caused by a chemical — ergot — in a fungus that grows on rye, wheat and some grasses. People called it Saint Anthony's Fire because of the painful burning sensation it caused in the limbs, but it has other symptoms, such as vertigo, vomiting, a crawling sensation on the skin, diarrhoea and hallucinations. There was an outbreak of ergotism as recently as 1951 in a small town in France, but it is not common now because bakers use preservatives to keep bread from spoiling.